THE LITTLE M

THE LITTLE MOVEMENTS

SAMUEL BURROWS

ROMAN *Books*
www.roman-books.co.uk

ISBN 978-93-83868-02-5

Typeset in Adobe Garamond Pro

First published in 2015

1 3 5 7 9 8 6 4 2

British Library Cataloguing in Publication Data
A catalogue record for this book is available from the British Library.

Publisher: Suman Chakraborty

ROMAN Books
26 York Street, London W1U 6PZ, United Kingdom
Unit 49, Park Plaza, South Block, Ground Floor, 71 Park Street, Kolkata 700016, WB, India
2nd Floor, 38/3 Andul Road, Howrah 711109, WB, India
www.roman-books.co.uk | www.romanbooks.co.in

Printed and bound in India by
Repro India Ltd

For Steven and Tina Burrows

I

SARAH AND SIMON

2001: TABLEMATS

The emptiness came from within, pressing itself outwards like an illness. He finished his meal to the faint sound of a television in another room, filling himself in one sense but failing to fill the real emptiness, which was cold and uncomfortable.

'You coming through?' Sarah said, walking from the room the sun had been on most of the day.

He was at the dining room table, his empty plate pushed to one side, looking at a tablemat with the lost concentration of someone staring at an open fire.

'Well?' she said.

'Someone's been messing with these,' he said.

'What are you on about?'

'These,' he said, pushing the tablemat to the other side of the table.

'Careful, you'll only make it worse,' she said, walking over. She leaned across the table to collect the tablemat, making a stretching noise, which made him look away.

The string was coming undone and unfastening the thin wooden sticks of the tablemat. 'I can fix this,' she said.

'Probably not,' he said.

‘Things don’t last forever,’ she said.

He groaned.

She said, ‘How long have we had them anyway? When was Crete? How long did you expect to have them? When Jess grows up and leaves us? When we’re collecting our pensions?’

‘It was probably her.’

‘We’ve had them years, Simon. Loosen up, will you?’

‘Don’t make fun of me. It’s not like we have many nice things as it is.’ *Nice things.* He wished he’d said something different.

‘Bloody hell,’ she said. ‘Over tablemats. Of all things.’

‘Of all things.’

‘Are you coming through or not?’ she said.

She returned to the warmer room, leaving the door open behind her, and she watched the television. Thinking of the cold draft, he came through and sat beside her.

‘Going to change out your suit?’ she said.

‘No point now,’ he said, looking at his watch.

He turned the television down. ‘Her bedroom’s above, remember?’

‘Didn’t say anything,’ she said.

On television was a French documentary about gleaning. He tested his knowledge of the French language by reading the subtitles. She had some papers on her lap, planning a few lessons for the week.

‘No marking?’

‘No.’

‘Want something to drink?’

‘All right,’ she said.

She came back a few minutes later with two glasses of white wine.

'Okay?' he said.

'Just went to the toilet first,' she said.

'Jess asleep?'

'Didn't check.'

'We'd know if she wasn't,' he said.

'Put something else on. What's gleaning anyway?'

'Collecting leftover crops.'

He went through a few channels until they both agreed there was nothing on. He put the documentary on again.

We pick from the ground before the crop goes bad. This is the old way, which is sadly no longer with us. The machines the farmers use now are too efficient. They leave us little to glean, and, anyway, today is the time of waste, the era of waste, throwing away. It can be seen in the cities, the overflows. In fact, this is the only gleaning of this generation. You've seen them, the tramps. They glean the bins of the cities. But the perception is different. The perception is negative, dirty. People like us, we're not afraid to get our hands dirty or to be criticised for it. Hands can be washed.

'What did you have?' she said.

'What are you talking about?'

'Dinner.'

'You know what I had. Pasta.'

'From Monday?'

'Yes,' he said.

'Wants throwing out. Don't eat it tomorrow. Won't be any good.'

'I finished it,' he said.

'Suppose there wasn't much left, was there? Should've brought the bottle in, shouldn't I? Think you'll want another?'

He nodded.

I gleaned with my mother. We worked hard all day together and then we went home and drank coffee together. Do you see that building? It's a farmhouse. I was born there and I'll die there.

She came back in with the bottle and some chocolate.

'Dessert,' she said.

'That's Jessica's, isn't it?'

'I'll get her more tomorrow.'

He made a noise to show disapproval. She opened the chocolate and put a piece in her mouth.

'Don't you want any then?'

He reached for the chocolate but she moved away.

'Don't,' he said.

'It's Jessica's, you said. We shouldn't be eating this.'

He went for it again so she moved it farther from his reach, and when he tried harder she sat on the chocolate.

'It'll melt. Don't be silly,' he said.

'All right, here you go,' she said.

They shared the chocolate and drank all of the wine. If they'd had another bottle, they would have drunk that too.

'What did you call Wednesday the other week? I can't remember. You know, someone at your work said something about it,' she said.

'Hump-day,' he said.

'That's right. Hump-day,' she said, playing with over-pronouncing the *p*. 'Weird, isn't it?'

'I'd never heard it before,' he said.

'I'm tired,' she said.

'It's the wine.'

'Maybe it's something else.'

He wondered what he was meant to say to that, or if she

wanted him to say anything. As well as he knew her, he couldn't tell sometimes.

'Want a lager? There's some in the fridge,' she said.

'Shouldn't really. We'd just be drinking for the sake of it, don't you think? I've had enough, but you have one if you want.'

'I'll have two if I want.'

'That's not what I meant.'

'Anyway, I suppose you're right. I've got to be up early too.'

He took their empty glasses, the empty bottle of wine, and the empty chocolate wrapper out to the kitchen. He washed the glasses with his dinner plate and cutlery, recycled the bottle, and threw away the wrapper. On his way back to the living room, he looked at the fraying tablemat again. The emptiness returned. He looked at the tablemat for about half a minute, a slight wine swing affecting his balance. He thought about the day they bought the set of tablemats and how sunny it was. He realised that he wasn't thinking of a particular day, but of the holiday in general. It struck him that he couldn't remember anything specific about Crete: there was sun, they ate well, they swam. But he remembered the flight home better than anything that happened on the holiday, and he remembered unpacking. He remembered thinking that they shouldn't have started to use the tablemats in the house, but what good were they if they weren't to be used?

'It's not like they're special,' she once said, to which he said nothing. He didn't want to tell her they were, since she was so sure they weren't. A couple of days later, she said, 'If we don't use them, what will we do with them? You want to hang them on the wall?'

He sighed, stopped thinking about Crete, and returned to

the living room. Her cheeks were blushed from the wine. She still sat like she used to sit, playfully, her legs tucked under herself. She smiled.

'That tablemat is ruined,' he said.

She breathed in and put her hands over her face. 'Oh no,' she said. 'What are we going to do? The tablemat! The tablemat!'

He felt like as though he might laugh, but it didn't quite happen.

About fifteen minutes later, she said, 'How many tablemats did we buy?'

'You know how many. Four.'

'Okay, so we had four tablemats. Now one is damaged. And how many do we have in our family? We have three. So why don't we throw it out? We've got three and three is all we need.'

'Another one will only go soon.'

She felt like strangling him. 'Well, when the second one goes and there's only two left you can always divorce me. So there'll be a mat for you and a mat for Jess. And hopefully the two mats last until Jessica moves out so you can throw the third one out the day she leaves home. And you'll be left with the final mat, which will be enough, because there'll just be you: Simon and his beloved tablemat. You'll have to take care of that one though, because when that one goes—the final one—I don't know what will happen. Christ, it's a tablemat, Si. Just a tablemat.'

Gleaning was very beautiful. 'We would see the gleaner, tramping along, gathering the relics of what falls behind the reaper.' You recognize it?

Du Bellay?

Du Bellay. Yes. Du Bellay.
It's wonderful that you know it by heart.
I know everything I love by heart, every little piece.
You keep it with you.

1976 & 1998: FATHER'S DAY

1976

A person called a careers adviser came into Simon's school and used the morning assembly to give a talk. It was all about this new thing called a career. It seemed like the most important word the pupils had ever been told. Career. It sounded strange to say. The word started strong, but trailed off into nothing like a slow illness with its soft and unsure *er* ending. The advisor closed the assembly by telling each student to think carefully about what they liked doing. She said she would try to visit each classroom by the end of the day to speak to each student individually.

Simon remembered thinking that he liked riding his bike, he liked the coast, and he liked some sports, but he had the feeling that the careers adviser meant something different. He had no idea what she'd asked him to think about. He felt stupid, because the question couldn't have been simpler, could it? When she came into his classroom, he felt his face becoming a little red. He punched himself in the leg. The careers adviser took a seat in the corner of the room. She was going to talk to each student in front of the entire class. Simon tried to think again about what he liked doing. He thought of subjects and activities in which he had no interest, like science or reading, because he didn't know what she wanted him to say. She started to speak to the pupils in alphabetical order. Simon divided his concentration between the maths his teacher had set and the quiet conversation in the corner of the room. It was obvious Mr Johnson was listening to each conversation too. He set maths when he didn't want to teach.

Simon couldn't concentrate on the maths, but Mr Johnson didn't check answers anyway. Simon was next. Abby's talk lasted eleven minutes. What were they talking about? If he knew, he would have said the same, word for word.

He sat opposite the adviser.

She said, 'Do you like working in large groups, small groups, or by yourself?'

'Don't mind.'

'Do you think of yourself as a leader?'

'Not really,' and she accurately noted that he was no leader. He felt warm. He calmed himself by thinking about her question: *A leader? Leaders were adults, weren't they? Was Abby a leader?*

'Would you rather design something or build it?'

Simon turned from Abby to face the careers woman again. She was waiting for an answer. He wanted to ask what it was that needed designing or building because that made a difference, didn't it? He said he'd rather design because he didn't want to ask a question. He was sure his classmates could hear. Mr Johnson had moved closer. The classroom was quiet. Simon was sure he was wrong.

'Do you like to be outside?' she said.

'Yes,' Simon said, smiling.

'In the cold too?'

'Don't know.'

'Try to think.'

'I don't know.'

Even Simon knew the adviser didn't know what to say. He wanted to tell her not to worry about him. In a perfect world, he would say, 'Don't worry,' and she would say, 'Okay,' and he would leave the table, sit back in his chair, and she would speak to someone else. But he couldn't say anything.

'What does your father do?' the adviser said and Simon wasn't at all worried anymore about the concept of a career or the conversation he was stumbling through. He didn't think of his classmates. His shyness left as her question registered. *My father?*

Mr Johnson spoke with the adviser outside the classroom for a minute. When she returned to her table, it was someone else's turn.

Simon sat by himself that lunchtime, watching the playground. There were a group of boys who liked to play a game they called 'cops and robbers'. One team would square up against the other and they would pretend to shoot each other. When Simon played with them and got shot, he went down as soon as possible. He sometimes even tried to get shot first so that everyone would see him dying. But it didn't matter if no one saw him; he still enjoyed it. Some of his friends refused to go down, claiming they hadn't been shot, but not Simon. He closed his eyes, felt the sun or the rain, and forgot himself. He stayed there for ages, pretending to be grass. He once opened his eyes to an empty playground, his friends having gone back to class. And another time he woke in the road.

His friends asked if he would play after school. Simon said he would, but went home instead. He slept a while, before waking in the dark and leaving his bedroom to find his mum.

'Do you want something, Mum?' he said. 'Mum. Mum.'

'Yes dear,' she said in a voice like she was speaking in her sleep, and then, in the same voice, 'Don't shout, dear.'

It was as though she was speaking with letters that had been used too many times and needed changing.

'Mum?'

'Yes.'

He said, 'What do you want then? Do you want something to eat? I'll cook you something.'

'Don't even think about touching that oven.' Her voice made him look away. Her voice reverted back, though, to the sleep-like sounds when she said, 'I'm not hungry, dear.'

He looked at her again. He didn't know what to do. He thought of others who had died. He had known a boy who got hit by a bus and died on his way to school. There was a girl who had become ill and died. One of his grandparents had died.

'Oh my, it's ten. You should sleep,' she said.

'Don't want to.'

'School tomorrow, come on.'

He shook his head. She looked as though she might speak until the silence, or something in the silence, made her eyes go back to the look that made Simon nervous. Simon concentrated on the sound and the movement of the second hand on the clock. Did the hand move at the same time he heard the sound? He couldn't be sure. He may have heard it before he saw it. But if he had to give an answer on which his life depended, he would have probably said that the sound and the movement happened at the same time. After testing another sixty times, he remained unsure.

'Don't like clocks. Do you, Mum?'

'What's that?'

'Don't like clocks. They annoy me.'

'Throw it away then,' she said.

'Don't mean that clock. I mean all clocks.'

'Throw them all away then, I don't know.'

Simon shuffled in his chair to avoid facing the clock. After a while, he decided that clocks weren't so bad after all and he repositioned himself back to where he was, an audience to the clock. Nothing was boring anymore, or boredom meant something else now and he had yet to experience it. It was waiting somewhere for him, perhaps, waiting for its name. Boredom used to be waiting in line for gingerbread at the bakery, or sitting in school. Watching a clock would have certainly been boring a couple of weeks ago.

It was almost a new day outside. He watched his mum, searching for some kind of sign that she wanted him there. He thought it was best to stay, but he wasn't sure. Her face was more like a shadow than a face.

He was sure she was never going to speak again until she spoke. 'You staying up with me then?'

'I'm not tired.'

'You don't have to say that,' she said.

'I'm hungry.'

'Come on,' she said, and they went into the kitchen. 'It's late.'

Simon wanted to know the time. He rushed back into the living room, saw that it was ten past one and nineteen seconds, twenty seconds, twenty one seconds, and then returned to his mum.

'You know my favourite song, don't you?'

Simon shook his head and, as if that wasn't enough, said, 'I don't know. You listen to lots.'

'*Love Me Tender*, and it's very important you remember that.'

'Why?' he said.

'Just remember.'

She turned and looked in the cupboard. Her shoulders lowered and he thought she was crying again.

'Can we have mushrooms on toast?' he said.

'You don't want more than that?'

He shook his head.

'Okay,' she said, collecting the ingredients.

She said, 'Forget about my song. You don't need to know.' The mushrooms were warming in the pan. 'If you eat, you'll be full. And then you'll sleep.'

'Don't think so,' he said.

'It's true.'

'Are you eating?'

'I'll eat,' she said.

She let him butter the toast. He used a lot of butter because the mushrooms were almost black. They sat at the table. Her mouth was full but he couldn't start eating until he admitted something. 'Sixteen days ago I stole,' he said.

'What did you steal?'

He had stolen before and been caught, but this was different. 'Money, from you.'

It was as though she had leapt across the table because in no time at all she was standing over him, smacking him where she could. Some strikes hit him awkwardly on the neck or the collarbone, but a couple hit his face.

'Never steal. Especially from your mother.'

He was crying but, in a way, he felt better. He couldn't understand or put words to it, but it was there, as clear as the outline of her hand on his face. Even her wedding ring was visible, under his right eye.

1998

'Happy Father's Day,' Sarah said in a high-pitched voice, holding Jessica in front of her head. 'Take her a minute.'

He held Jessica and said, 'What time is it?' but Sarah had already left the room.

She returned a few minutes later with two plates of fried mushrooms on toast. The toast and mushrooms were almost burnt, how he liked it. 'Look what Jess and I made. Your favourite. Happy Father's Day.'

He couldn't work out if Sarah was now wishing him a happy Father's Day or had forgot to put on her baby voice. Sarah repeated herself and he realised that she was indeed wishing him a happy Father's Day. He said, 'Thank you, and thank you for the breakfast too.'

When they finished eating, Sarah reached by her side of the bed. She handed Simon a carrier bag. 'From us.'

He opened the card first. Within a mess of coloured crayon, he could see a black outline of *Daddy*.

'This is nice. Thank you.' He looked at the cover. It read: *best dad in the world*. There was a cartoon dad holding a baby girl. The dad's hair was the wrong colour. Simon folded the card backwards and stood it on his bedside table to display the inside of the card. He opened the small present, a bar of his favourite chocolate. 'Thank you.'

'It's nothing.'

'Probably more than I'll get by the time she's thirteen.' They had joked before about what it would be like when she reaches her teens. It was starting to get old.

'I'll make a pot of tea,' he said.

Two cats were fighting under their bedroom window. He walked downstairs and opened and closed the front door, hoping to scare them. He made a pot of tea, listened to some radio news, and took two cups upstairs.

'You always forget,' she said.

'What?' he said, and realising she referred to the playing radio, added, 'Hold on,' leaving the room.

'Should call my dad soon,' she said, when he returned.

'Still feeding those cats?'

'Not since you told me not to.'

'Good,' he said.

'We should get out and do something. Oh, you seeing your dad today?'

'Why did you say it like that?'

'I'll come again if you want,' she said.

'I'll go later. Should do.'

She finished her tea and put the cup on her bedside table. The sound of it made him flinch. She felt he had exaggerated the flinch to show he was annoyed at her for saying 'seeing your dad.' He often said he was *going to see his dad*. Why couldn't she? Sarah didn't want to use the word grave either if she didn't have to.

'I'll call dad now,' she said, picking up Jessica and moving her closer to Simon.

'Send him my regards,' he said.

'Always do,' she said. She dialled from the landline and

sat on the bottom step of their stairs, waiting for him to answer.

He answered, 'Oh fuck it, fuck it. Hello Sarah, how are you? Wait a minute, please. Fuck it.'

Sarah held the phone half an arms length away and waited until she couldn't hear him anymore. The tone of his swearing told her nothing was wrong. It was the same swearing she heard for a dropped glass or when England lost a wicket.

'Sarah, are you there? Hello.'

'Yes, I'm here. What was all that about?'

'Spilt something.'

'What?'

'Some coffee, nothing to worry about. How are you? Okay?'

'I'm fine, just calling to say happy Father's Day. Did you open my card?'

'Oh, yes, I've got it here to open. Was going to open it soon.'

'You sound busy.'

'Just wiping up this bloody fucking mess.'

'No, I mean to have not opened my card yet.'

'Bloody hell, Sarah. It's not as if it's late. It's still morning.'

'I wasn't saying I was mad. I was just kind of asking if you were busy. So, how's work?'

'It's okay, same as usual. I suppose I am busy really, to answer your question.'

Simon walked past with Jess in his arms. Sarah moved out of the way, and when Simon and Jess were in another room, she said to her dad, 'So you've been working today, this morning?'

'Was going through some things, nothing too heavy. You know.'

'Your work get wet?'

'A little.'

'Sorry about that.'

He said, 'At least my card didn't get wet, right? That's far more important. I'll open that when we get off the phone. Looking forward to that. So you're okay then? Work's okay, and Simon?'

'Everything's good. Simon sends his regards. He said to say that.'

'That's nice. Tell him I said hi, won't you?'

'Promise me you won't work too hard.'

'I know, I know.'

'What are you doing today apart from work?'

'Nothing special,' he said.

'Look, I can hear you're distracted. How much did you spill?'

'The whole pot. Look, let me sort this out and then call you back, okay?'

'I'll call later on. I think we're heading out.'

'Okay. Goodbye, love.'

She hung up the phone and came through to where Simon and Jess were sitting. She told Simon about the coffee and he laughed.

'You don't find it funny?' he said.

'He didn't even ask about Jess.'

'Well, he was busy, like you said.'

'Busy?'

'The coffee.'

'Maybe,' she said.

'I would like you to come with me today,' he said.

'Sure?'

'Of course.'

They put Jessica in the car and left. Sarah kept to topics on the news. They talked about two university students who were in hospital after climbing somewhere in the peak district and getting themselves in trouble. And they talked about an actor who had died. He was eighty-six. Sarah said she hadn't seen a film of his, but Simon said she had and he described the film at length until she said she remembered. They parked at the church and spoke about how well behaved Jessica was in the car. 'Except for that one time,' Sarah said. 'Those fifteen minutes.' They thought she would damage herself, such loud screams for little lungs. They were often frightened of that throughout the first few weeks.

They stood together at the grave and Simon rested the flowers he had bought.

'Take her,' Sarah said.

He held Jessica and looked again at the gravestone, focussing on the dates more than anything else.

'This is the first time for her, isn't it?' Sarah said.

'I brought her here last month when you were at your mum's.'

'I didn't know.'

'I didn't tell you?'

'No,' she said.

'Sure I didn't?'

'Yes.'

'You seem annoyed I didn't tell you.'

'I'm not. I just don't know why you wouldn't have said.'

They drove back and sat in the living room together.

'Something to drink?' she said.

'I don't mind,' he said.

'How about now?' showing him a packet of his favourite loose-leaf tea.

'If you want some,' he said.

'Not enjoying today, are you?' she said.

'Not really.'

'Wanted to make it special for you. Shouldn't I have?'

'It's not you.'

'I feel silly. It's your first Father's Day, that's all. You treated me on Mother's Day. Shall I not bother next year? I don't mind. I'm not saying I mind. We can wait until she's old enough to choose whether she wants to buy us presents. It's not like it's Christmas or anything. My dad hardly cares about it. He didn't even open my card.'

'I promise it's not that. Next year will be different.'

'What is it then? What's wrong?' she said.

When he started speaking, she could tell from the tone that this was a subject he didn't want to speak about. He said, 'I realised today I'm older than my dad ever was. Isn't that weird? I know he died young. Even at the time, I knew he was young and I knew I'd be older than him one day, or at least I hoped I would. But now I'm older, I feel strange. It feels wrong.'

'I'm sorry. That didn't cross my mind.'

'Or mine, until I woke with it. And it felt like it was him telling me. Like he'd been waiting for this. I'm older than he was, but he's still my dad. Or was. It's weird. You shouldn't be sorry. It wasn't as though I even thought about it. It was just there, with me this morning. I've been older than him for a few months, but I only realised it today. When I woke, I could smell soil. For some reason, everything in that smell told me.'

'Why soil?'

'I don't know, his grave? But I don't know. It doesn't matter, does it?'

He felt uncomfortable with what he'd said. It didn't express exactly what he meant. Although the detail of the soil at one time felt significant, he now wasn't sure. If he'd said he woke and saw his dad's coffin in the room, which is something he wasn't sure he saw or not, would it have given her a more accurate account of how he was feeling? He felt he should have said that he woke and his dad was sitting on the edge of the bed. That's what it felt like. He felt as though his dad had been waiting for this day to tell him something. But it was the soil that meant something to him so that's what he said.

His mother's death came to mind. Hers was different than his. A short illness and that was that. He was thirty. He had a job, a flat, and Sarah. He concentrated on the engraved pattern of ivy in the vicar's cassock throughout the funeral service. It was the only thing he could think of doing. For some reason, blinking helped to uncover memories, and then he would try to not cry and then cry. For two months before her death, Simon's mother had been asking him to repaint her front door. He'd painted it the wrong shade, she said. She said she wouldn't have minded if it was the back door. But it was the front and it was important, she said.

'People see this door, it matters,' she said.

He said he would get round to it. He promised to do it and he thought he meant it. He concentrated on the engraved pattern instead.

'What does it mean? Sarah said.

Simon shrugged his shoulders.

‘Why soil?’ she said.

‘I can’t tell you.’

He thought about the idea of heaven before thinking of something else.

1985: LITTLE MOVEMENTS

The light breeze toyed with the thin tent's flysheet and it was somehow like music. They listened to its movement like the first crackles of a record.

'Simon.'

'Yes,' he said.

'Goodnight,' she said, moving her face close to his and kissing him.

He could feel her watching him.

'I want you to know me,' she said.

The small space of his tent made her sentence feel important. She wondered where the importance of what she had said came from: that she *wanted* him to know her (and she had never wanted this before), or she wanted *him* to know her (and she had never wanted anyone else before), or she wanted him to *know* her (and she had never wanted to be known before).

Not wanting to get lost in thought, she said, 'Camping's more comfortable than I thought it'd be.'

'I told you, didn't I?'

'I'm very happy,' she said.

'Do you realise that's the second time you've said that today?'

'Sorry,' she said, lowering her head into the neck of her sleeping bag.

'Don't be sorry.'

'I know you want to sleep, I'm sorry.'

'It's okay,' he said.

She thought again of him in that tree earlier. Why did it still make her nervous?

'This is the first time I've slept in a tent,' she said.

'Nice, isn't it?'

'It really is. Do you know what I'm thinking?'

'No. What are you thinking?'

'That we should go somewhere, another country, and stay in a tent together, like this, you know, after my training.'

'I was thinking the same,' he said.

'You were?'

'I was.'

Simon, Sarah, the music of the light breeze. There was nowhere else to look, nothing else to listen to.

He woke with a headache, not saying anything of it until the second time she asked what was wrong.

'You should've said earlier,' she said. 'I've got pills.'

He took two with a short sip of water. She told him to finish the water. She said he would feel better soon and encouraged him to eat more breakfast. They shared a small loaf of bread, tearing off handfuls before covering it in raspberry jam.

'Just need a coffee,' she said.

'You or I?' He wondered if she meant he needed the caffeine for his headache.

'Me.'

'We'll get one from the main bit,' he said. 'And we could fill the flask.'

She had coffee, him tea. There were ten chairs, seven of which were taken, so they stayed together, close to the counter. After they finished they asked for their flask to be filled with coffee, but the girl said it wouldn't fit under the nozzle. So they bought two coffees and filled it themselves. Sarah pocketed some sugar packets.

'Will you be staying tonight?' the girl said.

'Yes,' he said, opening the door for Sarah.

'Didn't we already say?' Sarah said when they were outside.

'I think that was a different girl,' he said.

'You sure?'

He said he wasn't sure and let out a small laugh.

'Those must have been the people I heard last night,' she said.

'I didn't hear anyone last night.'

'Early evening I mean, not last night.'

'Can't remember. Anyway, we'll be walking away from everyone today. I bet we don't see anyone where we're going,' he said.

'Take it a bit easy. Can't walk too far,' she said.

'Nice to be alone though.'

The higher they walked, the more he wanted them to be alone. A thought occurred to her, but it was too big to fully hold. She concentrated on her walking, the slight pain in her thighs, and the noise of her camera bouncing from her chest with each step. After a deep, dry breath, he said, 'Imagine we were different people—in appearance only—each time we met. So imagine I'm outside the post office, like usual, waiting for you.'

'I'm not always late,' she said.

'But I'm always early. So I'm waiting. I know I'd recognise you however you looked. It's just this feeling I get when I see you. Do you think you'd see me?'

'You'd be the one standing outside the post office.'

'No, really,' he said.

'Of course. There's this way you hold yourself. I can't work out if sometimes it's because you feel awkward or because you feel restless, but I'd know it was you if I saw it. I've never seen it in anyone else.'

'If I were a different person I'd hold myself differently.'

'Maybe I wouldn't notice then,' she said.

'I'm not explaining myself properly.'

'I'm thirsty,' she said, so they stopped to drink.

'It's confusing,' he said.

'Why do you want to be alone so badly?'

'No reason. It'd just be nice, don't you think?'

'Thought you might be proposing,' she said.

'Wasn't planning to.'

They both laughed. There was an emptiness in his stomach.

He said, 'We're alone now, aren't we?'

She nodded.

'So marry me. Let's get engaged.'

'What?' she said.

'I don't want anyone else. Do you?'

'Of course not.'

'Then will you marry me?'

Getting on one knee crossed his mind, but it didn't feel natural; it didn't feel like something he would do.

'So you *were* planning this?' she said.

'Didn't cross my mind until now. Until you brought it up. So it's your fault. So, how about it?'

'Okay. Yes,' she said.

'Okay.' He kissed her.

'You were planning this?' she said, laughing.

'Honestly, I wasn't,' he said. 'Haven't got a ring, have I? I'll buy one though, I promise. And soon.'

She was smiling as though she suspected Simon had planned it, so he said, 'I didn't plan this. But it makes it better, don't you think?'

'It is better.'

They held hands until the path became too steep. They arrived at the peak and sat there until the wind became too much. The descent was more difficult, and this surprised her. It hurt her thighs a lot. Simon said his thighs hurt as well and this made her feel better. She could now imagine becoming used to camping and walking. Every now and then she would remember they were engaged and smile. By the time they reached the tent and sat down to eat, she fully acknowledged it was the right thing to do. They ate together and rested in the tent. They lay close together. She hoped he wouldn't change his mind. They were both drifting in and out of sleep. She woke and started going through her bag.

'What it is?' he said. 'What do you want?'

'My torch. Weren't asleep, were you?'

'Here,' he said, handing her his torch.

'Need to read for a bit. I'm not tired.'

She read and he started to write in his notebook. She had never seen him write anything before aside from shopping lists and music playlists. It made it difficult for her to concentrate.

She read slower than usual and waited for him to finish. He was still.

She said, 'What were you writing?'

'This,' he said, handing it to her.

She read: *This is about noticing the little things you do and reacting to them without you noticing. It's effortless. I'm reacting almost unconsciously. This is how we move. We react to each other in little movements no one else notices. You might lower your eyes a fraction and I might understand that. So I touch your arm and it's what you wanted. So you lean into me and we stay still for a moment. We move again when we want to move, somehow speaking without words. We continue like this. Who else would notice the sign of your lowered eyes? Even if they noticed them, they wouldn't know what it meant, or how to respond. But I know you.*

She couldn't think of what to say except, 'What is it?'

'Do you like it?'

'I love it, of course I love it. It's the best thing anyone's ever said—or should I say written—about me. It's the only thing. Nobody has ever written for me before. So it's everything. But what is it? A poem?'

'No,' he said, almost laughing at the idea. 'Just felt like writing.'

'It's so nice,' she said.

'It's true.'

'But the reacting part; I'm not going to believe you without a test,' she said.

'I'd expect nothing less,' he said.

She crossed her body with her left arm and raised her left eyebrow a fraction. 'So?' she said.

'That's easy. You want me to kiss you.'

'Okay,' she said and sat in a neutral position again, before moving her left foot repeatedly in a sideways motion while parting her lips a little. 'And now?' she said.

'That means you want me to kiss you too.'

'Right both times. Well done. I want this. Can I keep it?' she said, holding his writing in her hands again.

He nodded. She didn't want to fold it but had no choice. She folded and put it inside her book. Now that there was physical evidence of their love, something tangible she could actually hold in her hands, it was more real. She was struggling to keep hold of one thought for longer than a few seconds.

He said, 'In ten years time, where do you want to be? What do you want to have done?'

'Don't know,' she said.

'You want to be a teacher. That's the first thing, right?'

'Of course.'

'Well, what else then?' he said.

'Why do you want to know?'

'I want to make sure it happens, *they* happen, your ambitions.'

'That's sweet, but I don't know. I'd like us to have a little house, somewhere nice.'

'Where's nice?'

'I don't know—not too close to a big town, not too cut off—and I want us to have good jobs, to be happy, to be healthy, to spend weekends cooking big meals while we drink wine and listen to music. And maybe have a family.'

'Okay, I can work with that,' he said.

'Actually, scratch that. I wouldn't mind us being cut off. It would suit your anti-social tendencies.'

'I'm not too bad.'

'I didn't mean it to sound bad, because it isn't bad. You know that I like your shyness. Will you remember what I want then? Sure you don't need to write it down?'

'I'll remember.'

'And what do you want?' she said.

'I don't know. Maybe surprises, nice ones. I'd like us to be able to still surprise each other.'

'Even though you already know all of me,' she said, opening her book and pointing to his writing.

'I know you, but you can still surprise me, I'm sure of it. I know it sounds like a contradiction, but it's true,' he said.

'A truth can be a contradiction. Who says it can't?'

The breeze picked up again, and it was like music.

1996: WHY I DON'T WANT IT

Sarah opened and read the letter, and she read the letter again. The second time slower than the first, but not because any deeper understanding was needed, but because after finishing the first read, she couldn't remember what she was going to do after checking the post. Sarah saw her slippers in the corner of the room so swapped her shoes for them. She wanted the bathroom but she didn't want to travel too far from the letter, so she returned to the table.

The letter lay on the table as if thrown there by a child. She felt a pain in her right hand. She must have been rubbing her index finger across the coarse underside of the table while reading. It was a habit she was aware of. The finger was red and there was a splinter. Her other fingers looked as white as paper. And they looked as lightweight too, as if they could be torn from her thin twig hand. She tried to work the splinter with her teeth before standing to find some tweezers. She got it first time. When she relieved the splinter, a little blood showed, the same shade as the finger from which it spotted. She kicked the nearest table leg and one slipper came off.

Simon entered. 'Why are you wearing only one slipper?'

'You have to notice everything, don't you?'

'Are you okay?'

'Before *hello* you have to point out the one thing that isn't as it should be, like every room you walk into is a spot the bloody difference cartoon. I'm going to the bathroom.'

'What is it?' he said when she returned.

She pointed to the letter. He looked over at it until she gave him permission. 'Yes, read it,' she said, and with a little too much force, frustrated her pointing wasn't permission enough. He took the letter and she watched him read. She looked for the little changes in his face, the angle of his eyebrows, a turning smile or frown, and the speed at which his pupils traced each line. Was he reading each line twice?

'Congratulations. Great news,' he said, but his response gave her nothing.

She concentrated on a short breath before speaking. 'I'm going to tell them I can't.'

'What? You deserve this.'

'I don't want it.'

He wanted to ask why she bothered applying for it, why they had spent weeks talking about nothing else, and why she attended the interview, but he said none of these and eventually said, 'I'll make us some tea.'

'I don't want it,' she said.

'I'm only making tea. You weren't talking about the tea, were you? You were talking about the job? You do want tea, don't you?'

'I'd like some tea.' She put her kicked slipper back on and sat at the table. She moved the letter around with the point of her index finger. He brought over two cups of tea and sat beside her. Some tea spilled. She moved to take the letter.

'Don't use that,' he said.

'I wasn't going to. I was going to read it again. As if you believed I'd use the letter as a wipe.'

He returned from the kitchen with a sponge and a dishcloth. He was happy to see her reading the letter. He thought she might change her mind and that all she needed was some time. Anyway, nothing needed to be decided or confirmed within a few weeks. The worst thing would be to pressure her into something she wasn't sure about. He took the sponge and dishcloth to the sink. She followed.

'It's nice our kitchen is warm,' he said.

'What do you mean?'

'The colours, other things too. It's a warm kitchen. Other people's kitchens are cold. They're white and big and cold.'

'I like our kitchen,' she said. She looked around the kitchen. She was thinking of all the different decisions people make in their lives and how not doing anything and not deciding anything is itself a decision to not do something or decide something. The motion never rests. She'd like to be a still image. She looked at the clock. The second hand of a clock can move in two different ways: on some, the second hand ticks awkwardly as if time is shoving it in the back to move it forward, but some second hands don't tick; they move with the fluidity of water. She was a second hand that ticked, and when she looked around at other people at work or in the high street, at her friends, or even Simon, she saw them moving like the other second hand, the fluid one. If a friend told her any of this, she would tell them not to worry. She would advise them that it was normal and that we all have these thoughts. But no friend had ever said anything like this to her. They were all fine.

'About the job then, what are you thinking?' he said.

'I don't know. It's difficult, don't you think? We haven't even caught up after Crete yet.'

'You'll be earning more.'

'But we'll have to move, and we don't know how much that'll cost. There'll be hidden costs. And I like this place. You were just saying how nice the kitchen is, how warm. I don't think I want to move.'

'You don't want to move?'

'You do?'

Simon shrugged his shoulders as he stood. He refused to say anything they had already spoken about at length. He poured more tea.

'It would be a pain, wouldn't it?' she said. 'You'd have to move branch.'

'They already said I could. We've spoken about this.'

She started to say something, but lost her way before the second syllable. He put her tea in front of her and moved to the other side of the room with his. Unsure if this was a new thought or the one that escaped her a moment before, she said, 'You know I love teaching, so to think about doing something different is . . .'

'I know it isn't that. We spoke about that before you even applied. You don't have to tell me specifically what it is, if there is a reason, but please stop making up reasons. It's not that far removed from lying to me.'

'You're saying I'm lying to you?'

'No, but I am asking you to only give me a reason if it really is the reason. That's all I'm saying. If you can't do that or you don't want to do that then it's okay, but I'd rather us be quiet.'

'Say something once, why say it again?' she sang in the style of David Byrne.

When Simon didn't respond, she walked to him. She rested her head on his back and she could feel him waiting for her to speak. She turned and looked at the coarse surface that lined the underside of the table. Although she was now in another room, the small splinters stuck out as clear as black letters on a white page, daring her to rub them again. It was strange she only suffered one splinter, she thought, lucky. She took a breath and said, 'I wasn't going to tell you yet. I was going to wait.'

'Tell me what?'

'I wanted to be sure. I don't want to let you down.'

'Just tell me,' he said, facing her.

'I'm pregnant.'

'Pregnant?'

'Yes,' she said, resting one hand flat on the kitchen side. Her stance looked uncomfortable. Her shoulders, uneven. She waited.

He smiled. 'I love you.'

It didn't feel like the first time he had told her he loved her but it felt new, as though the words had taken on a changed meaning. He opened the fridge and pulled a cork from a half-full bottle of white wine.

'It's not champagne,' he said, which would have sounded like an apology if not for the joy in his voice. He poured them each a small glass. They toasted to their future and drank. He could feel his smile high in his face.

'I'm frightened,' she said.

'I know. It's normal. I am too.'

'You don't look frightened.'

'I'm too happy to. Before today, the best news for us would have been your job offer. I didn't expect this. I'm frightened too, but we'll be okay,' he said.

He meant it. She was sure, in time, she would feel it too.

'You're everything to me,' he said.

Everything. He had said this before. She felt she should be smiling, but there was so much pressure. He put his arms around her and thanked her. Okay, she thought, things will be okay, but she was still frightened. She wanted to be invisible, if only for a moment. She thought of how she might do this. She thought of a pool of water and the reflection of her face. She would press her face into the water and sink into herself. That's how she would do it, if only it could be done.

2006: IT GETS BETTER

Sarah had said she was worried, but Simon said it was probably nothing—small after-school tears, he called them—and they should let her go to her room if that was what she wanted. Best to give her space, he thought. But when Jessica came downstairs, she said that for weeks now some girls wouldn't leave her alone.

'Come on,' he said.

'What? Where?' Jessica said.

'Help me buy dinner. We're going to cook.'

The three left together. They drove past the school playground on their way to the shop. There were too many crisp packets to count. Some were caught on the wire fence and some were moving freely. Some weren't crisp packets but chocolate and sweet wrappers, apple cores, banana skins, and dead leaves. They entered the supermarket. Jessica went to the magazine and book section.

'You can choose something small,' he said.

'One thing,' Sarah added.

Jessica had a colouring book in one hand and a bottle of glitter in the other. 'Do these count as one?'

'Two,' Sarah said.

'But there's no point having a colouring book without glitter and there's no point having glitter without anything to glitter on. You know that.'

'Okay, okay,' Sarah said, and Simon took the two items and put them into the trolley. They picked up a few bits they needed and asked Jessica what she wanted to eat.

'Pizza.'

On the way to the pizza, they stopped to look at the DVDs. Simon said, 'Remember when we saw that in the cinema a couple of months ago?'

'Yeah, *Robots*. Can I have it?'

Sarah looked at him and said, 'What did you think would happen?'

Simon said, 'She can have it.'

Jessica almost threw it into the basket.

'Careful,' Simon said.

They collected a couple of pizzas and drove home, an alternative route. Jessica put the DVD in the player and looked for the remote control.

'Wait until we're together,' Simon said.

'When dinner's ready,' Sarah said.

All three of them had pizza and they sat together. Jessica looked alright. With her favourite meal and a film she enjoyed, the world felt smaller and life became simple for ninety minutes. The film finished. As soon as the credits appeared, as if she had been thinking of it for the whole film, Jessica said, 'Don't even know why they're mean to me.'

'It happens to some of the girls at my school,' Sarah said.

'It happened to me,' Simon said.

Jessica turned and focussed on him, a movement like a startled cat. 'Really?'

'Yes.'

'What happened?'

He felt them both looking at him.

'I was tall as a boy. I'm tall now, of course, but I was taller, compared to the other boys, as a boy. I was one of the tallest in the year, every year. I never fought anyone, punched anyone, or wanted to. I wasn't tough and everyone knew this. It wasn't a bad thing and never in my life did I want to be considered tough, and even more than not wanting to be considered tough, I certainly never wanted to fight. But it only takes one person to start a fight. There was a period of about six months in my penultimate year of school, which felt closer to six years, when the oldest year in the school, well, some of the boys in the oldest year, took their turn to start a fight with me to look tough in front of their friends. Even at the time, as scared and as young as I was, I knew they were only doing this to look tough. Remember, I was very tall, often half a foot taller than those who fought me. Sometimes they would come up to me and give me a little push and then punch me in the mouth or the nose. I know my mum noticed a couple of bruises, but she never pushed me to tell her. She believed my lies and I was thankful at the time, but now I think I wish she'd got the truth out of me. I once told her I fell out of a shopping trolley that my friends and I were playing in. She couldn't have believed that. So, like I was saying, they'd punch me and my reaction would be to stay still on the floor. I knew that if I stood up they might hit me again. They never once kicked me. But the worst times, the absolute worst times that still upset me, were the times they would spend between ten and fifteen minutes talking to me before hitting me. They would invent things that I did and said and then ask me to apologise, which, of course, I did, and then they would laugh at me and continue with their stories. Sometimes the conversations went on for so long that I started to believe them myself. But some stories were silly. Some said I did things to their family and when I said *I haven't even met your family* with tears starting to form, well, you can imagine, everyone would laugh at me. I had friends but they never did anything. It's difficult though. These boys were older and one year is a significant period of time at school. I remember. My friends never even helped me stand up afterwards come to think of it. One of them, and this wasn't even a close friend of mine, once helped me clean the blood from my shirt.'

'Simon,' Sarah said.

He continued, 'But that was all the help I got. We can help you. You need to tell us everything that happens, like you did tonight. You're a good girl.'

'What was all that about?' Sarah said. 'Too much.'

He hadn't said all of what he was going to. He was going to tell her about the time they tried to push him in front of a car. He still dreamt about it occasionally.

'What was all that about?' Simon said, repeating Sarah's question as if standing himself to continue. 'Jessica, after all of this nonsense, you leave school and it finishes, just like that. It might seem a long way off, but I promise you it isn't. After school, you'll only see the people you want to see. The people who don't like or understand you will ignore you. They don't say anything. You speak to the ones you want. It gets better, darling.'

'Why did you tell her about all that violence?' Sarah said, almost without moving her lips.

Simon replied so Jessica could hear. 'Violence is bad and I don't understand it. I've never once hit anyone in my life, and I'm sure that I'll never. I haven't got it in me and neither has she.'

Simon had said all he wanted. He turned the television on and they watched the news and the weather and a film review programme. Jessica fell asleep on the carpet and Simon and Sarah noticed almost immediately.

'So what are we going to do?' Sarah said.

'Not sure.'

'We said we'd decide this week.'

'I haven't forgotten.'

Simon carried Jessica to bed, thinking of how little he knew, thinking how greatly his idea of the playground and the actual playground differed. He had imagined it as a clean place before today. It was as though a painter was working everywhere he wasn't looking. He turned away from his girl and cursed the painters.

'Do you think she believes us when we say everything will be okay?' Sarah said, when he returned.

'Who can say? I don't think I'd have believed. It's difficult.'

'I hope she believes us.'

'I do too, of course.'

'What if someone told us tonight that things would be okay? The bills, the mortgage, the rest. Would we believe?'

'Guess not.'

'I hope she believes us.'

'I'm going for a walk,' he said.

She looked up at him as he stood, maintaining eye contact.

'Back soon,' he said.

He walked to the school. There was a small barrier. He jumped over it to enter the playground. Within ten minutes, his hands were full of wrappers, and his sleeves were wet from the fallen rain. There was still more to collect. Although he wanted to be home, he wouldn't leave until he'd made a noticeable difference.

1984: I DANCE TO IGGY POP

Simon was late to meet Sarah, but he couldn't get the image of Van Gogh's *Chair* and Julie from his mind. The first time he visited the National Gallery, Van Gogh's *Chair* meant nothing. Simon saw it and moved to the next. It was hot and there were too many people around for him to take the time he wanted. But the real reason behind his disinterest was *Sunflowers*. It was his sole reason for visiting. Around twelve months after this visit he met Julie at the entrance of Hyde Park. Their letters were starting to become something, he thought. They had been meaning to meet for a while. He had cancelled a dental appointment to meet her. Julie was wearing a black skirt and a white shirt. She hadn't mentioned in her letters that her hair was blue. He preferred it pink. He asked which colour she preferred and she said, 'I suit neither of them equally.'

'I have lunch,' he said.

'Let's sit then,' she said.

They found somewhere.

'Don't want to walk too far,' she said.

He laid a picnic blanket and emptied two carrier bags. There were sandwiches, sausage rolls, crisps, pineapple chunks, oranges, and a bottle of red wine.

'It's too much,' she said.

Was she was trying to be polite? The entire afternoon lay in front of them. They started to eat. The sun shone sporadically between white clouds with thin dark grey edges, and that was about right. The important thing was that it didn't rain. He poured himself another wine, and offered her one.

She said, 'No, I can't. Time to get back. The things we have to do.'

'What? Back where?'

'To work. It was great to do this, finally.'

She put her arms around him. It sank in. He didn't say anything. She said, 'Didn't I say?' She was sure she had, and he was sure she hadn't. They spoke about this for a couple of minutes before she said she had to leave. 'Do you want to walk with me?'

'Not really,' he said. 'I'm still eating.'

She left after putting her arms around him one last time. Even at the time, he knew it was a pointless gesture. He sat and watched her walk until he could no longer spot her from the crowd, until she was the same as the others.

Simon decided, as he ate, to catch the train home. After he left the park though, he felt glad to be on his own and started walking towards Tottenham Court Road. He listened to buskers in the doorways of music shops playing the harmonica as though the sound had no right to emerge from something someone could hold in their hands. He walked through Covent Garden with the intention to stop and sit but didn't. He carried on through to Trafalgar Square and eventually ended up outside the National Gallery, to have another look at *Sunflowers*. But he stood in front of Van Gogh's *Chair* instead. He started to think of the last couple of years and how he couldn't feel comfortable in groups larger than two anymore. He'd told himself it was natural, but it was more than that. Only in front of the painting could he admit it to himself. He could see one or two signs of his nerves coming to him, as was often the case when he thought about them. The one piece of advice he had read to help cure his nervousness was to not think about it because thinking about it made it worse. What advice was that? He was sure his face was red and he was resisting the urge to bite his nails and the skin around his nails. The truth of his problem came to him—he started to look at the painting and he wanted, more than anything, to swap places with the pipe on the chair. Then he realised that the pipe was being watched and studied by over twenty people every one moment, and thousands of people over a week. People talking, sighing, frowning and smiling, looking straight at the pipe. So he no longer wanted to be the pipe. But he didn't want to be himself either. He had to be someone. This, in his opinion, perfectly explained everything.

And now, two years after this failed meeting with Julie, Sarah was waiting for him in a bar and he couldn't dislodge Van Gogh's *Chair* and Julie from his thoughts. He couldn't believe two years had passed. He had to at least turn up, didn't he? Sarah was expecting him. He took his coat from the back of a chair in the kitchen and left the house. Simon entered the bar, half an hour later than Sarah had suggested so that he wouldn't have to wait alone, and looked for Sarah in a crowd. He watched her dance to a song he was glad he recognised before walking to her.

'You came,' she said, one hand touching his side.

'But you invited me.'

'I know I did, but you might not have come.'

'It's just that you seem surprised that I'm here.'

Another person grabbed Simon's arm and he turned around. It was someone from his work, a person he hardly knew. A nod worked as hello and goodbye simultaneously. He turned back to Sarah and said, 'You seem surprised I'm here.'

'It's not that.'

'So you're not surprised I'm here? It's okay that I'm here, right?'

'What?'

'Loud, isn't it?' he said.

'Yeah,' she said. Her shouting was beginning to hurt him. The pain registered deep inside his ear. He hoped he wasn't hurting her when he spoke, but he assumed he probably wasn't. Her voice was higher, and this must have been the reason.

'Want to sit somewhere?' he said.

'There's nowhere to sit.'

Simon looked around to see she was right. He felt everyone's eyes on him. He worried about his clothes, the way he moved.

Sarah said, 'Annoying, isn't it?'

'The music?'

She laughed and said, 'No, that there's nowhere to sit. You don't like the music?'

'Hard to say; it's so loud I can't hear it.'

'But you like music, don't you?'

'Of course. We've talked about it loads of times,' he said.

She was no longer dancing. He was sure he was the reason. He started moving his arms. She smiled.'What?' he said, standing still again.

'Didn't say anything. Do you want a drink?'

'Suppose so. Would you like one?'

'I've got one,' she said.

'Okay, I'll get one then.'

He turned around, walked a couple of steps, and looked back at Sarah.

'Over there,' she said, pointing.

He couldn't remember why he looked back at her, but it wasn't for directions. Simon walked to the bar thinking that he didn't particularly want any alcohol. He thought people only drank in these kind of places to fit in. Pressed for an answer, he ordered a pint of lager and walked back to Sarah. He knew he could embarrass himself this evening. And he wouldn't only spoil his chances with Sarah, but he would also consider, once again, something that made him uncomfortable to think about, a thought he refused to give words to in the fear that it would feed it authority. He started moving. His feet tapped to the beat and he focused on trying to keep his arms moving, even though something deep within him resisted every movement. He was sure everyone was watching.

'This your favourite place?' he said.

'Don't you like it?'

'I like it.'

He wished he hadn't asked her that and he wished he hadn't said he liked the place, but he worried he had been silent for too long. He wondered if he should talk to one of the others around them. But what was there to say? He could think of nothing that wasn't cliché, or at least expected, and little else that wasn't dismissive of the music or the bar. When she said she wanted some fresh air, he could have kissed her. She told one of her friends something and they embraced. He looked at her bare shoulders as they left, her once pace in front. As they stood outside, she tried to not shiver. Her knees were shaking, but only a little, so she let them.

'You're not cold?' he said.

'I'm okay.'

'I think I might be leaving soon.'

She didn't say anything.

'It's pretty late, and you guys have been drinking all evening, well, not all evening, I didn't mean that, but you've been drinking more than me, longer than I have, but next time we can meet earlier, and then it'll be better, okay?'

'Are you leaving now? I thought you said soon.'

'I think I might leave now, yes, or in a bit. You must be cold, really.'

'But you won't come back inside?'

'I don't think so, no,' he said.

'Knew you didn't like it.'

'I didn't mean to lie.'

She looked at her feet, tapping in time to the music that came to them through the wall.

'You should go back to them, your friends. I don't want to spoil your night. I'd never want that,' he said.

'I like you though. I wanted to see you tonight, was looking forward to it. You're why I'm here, not them. It's you I like.'

'You said you come every week.'

'You're why I'm here *tonight*,' she said.

He thought about returning inside but he couldn't make himself want to. He said, 'Why do you like me? Sorry, don't answer that. I should leave. We can do something else another time, anything else.'

'I just like you.'

'Okay,' he said.

'Because, for starters, you don't even notice your good points.'

'Which are?' he said, too surprised to feel embarrassment.

'You're quiet in a good way and shy in a way I like. I don't know, but I think. You're not short, not weak. I can tell you're not. Also, I have this impression, these ideas, like thoughts, that if someone gave you something, you're the kind of person who would keep it. If someone gave you a flower, you'd take care of it.'

'Well nobody has ever given me a flower,' he said, as she stopped for breath.

'I could go on,' she said, her lower jaw making a shivering movement that he told himself he must remember.

'You should go back to them,' he said, thinking of the reason behind the little movement he loved—the cold.

'You don't know how to take a compliment. What I said doesn't make you happy at all, not happy one little bit?'

'Of course it makes me happy.'

'So be happy then,' she said.

'But I . . .'

'But you what?'

'It's strange to hear things like that.'

'We don't have to talk,' she said, before climbing his chest to kiss him.

'Are you going back to them?' he said.

'No.'

'Where then?'

'I'm coming home with you,' she said.

'You're coming home with me? This doesn't usually happen.'

She opened his hand and put hers inside. They walked. There was no conversation for ten minutes. Holding hands was enough. When he worked the lock with his key, she stood as close as she could to him. He felt her breasts close to his back. They entered. Sarah tried to concentrate on the room. The walls were plain. There wasn't much furniture except for a two-seat settee and a desk that didn't look like a desk but was used as one anyway. 'Can I get you a drink? I have white wine, I don't know if you like white wine, or lager, or there's water if you like,' he said.

The place looked clean and she remembered he probably hadn't expected a guest, so he must be a naturally tidy person, a quality she had hoped for and presumed. 'No, I'm fine, thanks.'

'Do you like white wine though, for next time, I mean?' He felt nothing of speaking as though there would be a next time.

'I'll share a bottle with you next time,' she said.

'Of white?'

'Yes, white.'

'But not this time, not now?' he said.

'I'm fine, but thanks anyway. Really, I'm fine.' She put her coat on the settee. There was no television she could see. There were a few books around, but not many. The carpet was thin and looked worn.

'Or would you like something to eat? I don't know.'

She might have laughed at this if she wasn't thinking of something else. She turned on a lamp and walked to turn off the main light. Because of the cold walk and the alcohol, her cheeks were a little blushed. It made her feel shy and she didn't want to feel shy this evening. 'No, thank you,' she said.

'Okay then, nothing to drink and nothing to eat. I don't know.' He sat in a chair by a small metal table, looking even more uncomfortable than he had done in the bar. She couldn't imagine him any other way. She wondered when he'd feel at ease. Two minutes, hours, months. When he asked what she was laughing at, she said she wasn't laughing at anything and let him think it was the drink.

'Do you like Iggy Pop?' he said, and she nodded without making eye contact. He walked over to a shelf and started looking. She stood near him and read aloud the names of the bands: 'Joy Division . . . The Smiths . . . Roy Orbison.'

'Anything you'd prefer?' he said.

'No, Iggy Pop's good.'

'Good, because I dance to Iggy Pop,' he said. 'Not really. I'm not going to dance.'

'Get my hopes up why don't you,' she said.

'*The Idiot* or *Lust for Life*?'

'*Lust*,' she said.

He played it. They talked about Bowie and Lou Reed and Iggy for a bit, of course, and after thinking about it for two or three songs, she made Simon stand with her. She danced so close to his chest that he felt conscious of his heartbeat. The song was *Tonight*. When the song sped up, they stayed slow. *Everything will be alright tonight.* He heard the opening bars of *Fall in Love with Me*, the final song, and he wondered what was going to happen after, but she had it all planned and he wouldn't have to decide anything.

1993: FEBRUARY 14TH

He rubbed his forehead, changed the channel.

'I was watching that,' she said, in an upright way that surprised him.

'I don't want to watch this. I can't watch anymore. Can you? Have you?' he said, realising she hadn't yet heard.

'Surely they were talking about it at school,' he said.

'What is it?' she said.

'I'm not sure you want to see it. No, you don't,' he said.

She took the remote control and changed the channel back. He knew she would, but even a few more seconds from knowing was important. They watched the rest of the news story in silence. Now she knew too.

'Two years old,' she said, two or three times.

He didn't say anything until the news finished. He started to explain why he tried to keep her from the story, but when he realised she wasn't listening, he stopped.

'Just two,' she said.

She rested her head back and looked at the raised pattern on the white ceiling. A few words circulated within her head: *carrier bag, batteries, infant.* Each word was different now.

And tomorrow would be something else too, something worse.

'We should have gone out tonight,' he said.

'How can you think such a thing?'

'You wouldn't have known until tomorrow.'

'Tomorrow. School,' she said, lifting her head. 'I can't go in.'

She was almost crying.

'After this,' she said.

He thought of encouraging her to go in, but he felt that any encouragement carried with it the danger that he might have somehow understood what had happened. If he had to work with ten-year-old children tomorrow he would struggle too. What only yesterday could have been a nostalgic and heart-warming sight—a couple of boys spending an afternoon together by a river—would now be something fearful. It would remain that way too. There was no understanding. There never would be.

'Tomorrow's Friday as well,' he said.

'What?'

'You know,' he said.

'You think if I found out tomorrow I'd be okay for Monday? You think I only need the weekend to feel normal again?'

He wished he had something different to say, but he said he didn't know. *Carrier bag, batteries, infant.* Everything was different. Simon thought of the first time he stole. It was chocolate from the village post office. He was ten. When his mother found the wrapper in his bedroom that afternoon, she led him to the post office. It was winter and his mother didn't even take the time to put on a coat. She walked cross-armed as if trying to protect herself from something. Throughout the short walk, he remembered asking her why they were returning. He wanted to hear her say it. She didn't say a word until they were inside the post office.

'My son has something to tell you,' were the words she chose.

Simon spoke when he realised that the man behind the counter knew why his mother and he were there.

'I stole.'

His mother paid for the chocolate and apologised more than once. She wasn't crying, but he remembered feeling that he shouldn't say anything as they completed the journey home. He had the feeling that any subject would make her cry immediately.

'You don't need to do things like that, Simon. I had to, but you don't. I don't know why you did that. I really don't,' she said before telling him she didn't want to see him until tomorrow. It was the only time she deliberately sent him to bed without dinner.

'How old were the children?' Simon asked Sarah.

'Ten.'

'Do you think we'll ever find out their names?'

'Probably not,' she said.

He asked her for a few more details and she answered each question. Soon enough, they were talking about it. She needed to. All they were doing was repeating what the reporter had said.

'You going in tomorrow?' he said later on.

She said, 'Well I have to, don't I? Can't let them down this late.'

It was no less terrible because they had spoken it aloud; in fact, it felt far worse and more confusing than it ever had done, and this is why she could face going in. Her children were nothing like those children. Even her little bastards were angels. They would never do anything like that.

'Anyway, I got you this,' he said.

'We said we weren't,' she said.

'I know, but I did anyway.'

She opened the plastic bag. A videotape: *It's a Wonderful Life.*

'When you said it was a shame we didn't watch it over Christmas, I wished I'd bought it for you, so I told myself to buy it for you next Christmas. But then I saw it in the shop the other day on sale. I bought it, since I was going to buy it for you anyway, for Christmas. Then I realised it was Valentine's Day and thought I might as well give it to you now.'

'Okay, thank you, but I wish I had something for you. I haven't even written you a card.'

'You get me a present next year if you want to, and I won't. How does that sound?'

'That sounds fair,' she said.

'Let's go to bed, shall we?'

'I want to walk. Will you walk with me?'

They left the house without either of them saying where they wanted to go. They walked. She tried to explain why she loved to see a town at night. He said he much preferred a view of the countryside and she said she liked that too, but there was something she couldn't put her finger on about how special a town was at night.

'Can you try to explain? I want to understand,' he said.

'Something about the lights all over the place, and the strange quiet of something that shouldn't be quiet, or a place that normally isn't quiet. It's like the town is sleeping. It sounds silly when I start talking about it. But I know what I mean.'

'I suppose I understand,' he said.

A bus without passengers came past. The light inside was a burnt orange.

She said, 'This has shaken me up a bit.'

'I know.'

'I can't figure if I've been naïve and things like this are bound to happen, or if this really is as terrible as it seems. And then I'm thinking whether I should even be questioning whether or not this is terrible because, let's face it, it is.'

'Have you been thinking more of the boy or his family?' he said.

'Neither. I've been thinking of the two ten year old shits.'

'You can't think of them. There'll never be any answers there.'

'But doesn't that make you think of them even more? I know that's illogical, but it's true, isn't it? Just because we tell ourselves not to think of something, it doesn't mean we stop, does it?'

'Sure doesn't.'

Another bus came past.

'That another 65?' she said.

'Was the first one a 65? I didn't see.'

'The first one was.'

'Was it?' he said.

'Yes. What about the last one though? Was that a 65?'

'I don't know.'

'Okay?' she said.

'I'd like to get home and go to bed,' he said.

'I know we have to, but don't you feel like it's wrong to just go on as normal?'

'How could it be?'

'I'm not saying it is wrong. I'm saying it feels wrong.'

'Let's go home.'

'Okay,' she said, and he said it too.

She saw Laura the following morning walking by the school office. She called her over and they walked towards each other. They met in the doorway. Mr Fletcher wanted to get through the door. 'Come in for a second,' Sarah said, trying to move her out of the way.

'Can't chat, heading to Miss Phillips with these,' Laura said, raising a handful of photocopies.

Sarah put her hands on Laura's shoulder and moved her into the hallway. Mr Fletcher entered the office.

Sarah said, 'Just wanted to see if you were all right, after that news story and all.'

'Horrible, isn't it?'

'I've never seen anything like it. But you're okay, right?'

'Are you?' Laura said.

'Look, you're in a rush. I'm all right. I'm fine. Catch up with you later on.'

'I'd like that. We could go for a couple of drinks.'

'Sure,' Sarah said, thinking it was one of those things she should still do despite not wanting to. Simon would encourage her to go if he knew. The last time she went out with Laura, they spoke about going to a London show together. It still hadn't happened and it was something Sarah still wanted to do. She would mention it later that evening. Half term wasn't too far away. She stood by the office trying to remember what it was she did during the last half term.

'When the bloody hell was last half term?' she said.

She shook her head before walking to where she was late to be. There was a lot to do and no time to be thinking of last half term or anything else.

1987: SOMETHING SHE WANTED

'I don't know what's wrong,' she said.

'It's okay. Rest,' he said.

He went downstairs, told work he couldn't make it in, and waited. He returned to the bedroom when he heard she was awake. He sat on the end of the bed.

'I thought you'd gone to work,' she said.

'I'm not going.'

'And what did they say about that?'

'Not much,' he said.

'I don't like you seeing me like this.'

'I don't like seeing you like this.'

'You know what I mean,' she said, covering her face with a pillow.

'We've been together long enough.'

'So it doesn't matter if I'm ugly? How sweet.'

'I'm not saying that, am I?'

'I almost didn't make it to the bathroom just now. Bring a bowl in.'

He found a plastic washing basin in the garage. He cleaned it and took it to the bedroom.

'Might get my dad to get me.'

'Long drive.'

'He won't mind,' she said.

'Not for him. For you. Can you imagine being in a car for over an hour? The way he drives too.'

'Don't know. I hate this.'

'If you want me to call him then just say. But I'm here and I'll take care of you. I won't go in tomorrow if you need me here,' he said and, when she covered her face again, added, 'And stop worrying about how you look.'

She made the decision to relax into his care, and soon fell asleep. Before sleeping, she was thinking about how nice it would be for them to be frozen in the house together, similar to the way people are sometimes snowed in, but different. It would be a time for the two of them. *But would we one day forget the ice was ever there? How much had we forgotten already?* She didn't like thinking about this, but she was overly tired and therefore desensitised. When she woke, he wasn't in the room. She called his name and he came in. She was sure she had something important to tell him, but once she spoke, she realised it meant little. 'How long was I sleeping for?'

He said she'd been asleep almost an hour and asked if she felt better. She said she did. The phone rang. Simon ran downstairs in thuds that pointed towards the tips of her headache. His voice travelled through to her sounding flat. Sarah pictured him in the kitchen, leaning his forehead against the wall, because that's where he stood when talking on the phone. She started to think about food and didn't feel well. He entered the room without her noticing and started to clean when she finished, with an old dishcloth he would soon throw away.

'Who was that? On the phone?'

'Nobody.'

'What have you been doing?'

'Had some lunch, a sandwich so there'd be no cooking smells.'

'Don't talk about food,' she said, one hand covering her eyes.

'You asked, I said. Sorry.'

'And don't be so defensive. I'm ill. Of course I'm gonna have a go.'

He laughed to himself and decided he had done enough scrubbing for the time being. She said she felt better so he ran her a bath. As he did, she held onto an image of a bed of grey stones, a strong urge to photograph them to make them look like water, their small bumps like waves. When she was in the bathroom, he tidied the bedroom. It was while changing the bed sheets to get the sick smell from the room, because he wanted to share the bed with her that evening, that he realised he was ready to think about children. But he might not mention it to her for a long time yet. It was one thing to realise he was ready but another to decide they were.

He sat on the fresh bed knowing she would soon finish her bath and come through to him. His readiness to have children was another commitment to spend his life with her, which was a permanence of this feeling, this waiting for her to come through to him. As he watched Sarah enter the bedroom, wrapped in her towel and smelling like herself again, he felt like picking her up. He may have done had she not been unwell.

'Why are you smiling like that?' she said.

'Like what?' he said, although he knew.

She smiled in almost the same way and got into bed. 'Take-away?'

'You don't want that. You're joking.'

'I'm not. I'm hungry.'

'You don't.'

'Maybe I don't, but I want something.'

'See how you feel in half an hour,' he said.

'Am I allowed a cup of tea at least?'

'Not sure that's a good idea.'

'Well I want something. I'm so fed up of water,' she said.

Simon held a smile in place until she looked at him.

She said, 'You're joking, aren't you?'

'Tea might not be a good idea.'

'You are joking. Stop it.'

'Okay, yes. I was joking. Of course I'll make you a tea.'

He went downstairs, made the tea, and carried up two cups. 'Joking aside, drink it slowly,' he said.

She took a sip.

'I've got some sewing to do,' he said.

'Give it here,' she said.

'Sorry,' he said, handing her a needle and thread.

She threaded it within a few seconds and said, 'Why are you sorry? It's not like I'm dying. I can sew. Really, you might as well give me what needs sewing. What is it?'

'A pocket on my coat has come away, but I'll do it,' he said, taking the threaded needle from her like he was taking a lit firework.

He sewed the small tear in his coat and they drank. 'How do you feel?'

'Hungry.'

'I'll make something. What would you like? Something cooked?'

She nodded.

'Do you want to come down with me or wait here? I don't mind.'

'I want to come down.'

'You sure?'

'I've been in here for what feels like a week.'

'Barely longer than a day.'

'I know that. I was telling you how it *feels*.'

'I know how it feels.'

'How *I* feel,' she said.

'I can guess how you feel.'

'Stop annoying me, please.'

'I'm sorry. I wasn't meaning to. I'll put the heating on,' he said, leaving the room and going downstairs ahead of her, as though half a minute would make a difference.

'We could make pasta,' he said, thinking of a wholesome meal.

'Anything but pasta. God, are you serious?'

'I forgot, I forgot, sorry.'

'I'm never eating pasta again. I swear you're trying to annoy me.'

He lifted a can of soup from the cupboard. She shook her head. She went to the fridge and took out some chicken. They grilled the chicken and made a thick tomato and pepper sauce to go with it. When it was almost ready, she opened the cupboard and said, 'There's no bread.'

He went upstairs for his coat, came down and walked towards the front door.

'What are you doing? Where are you going?'

'Bread,' he said and left. He came back some minutes later. She had served the dinner and was sitting at the table. He noticed the fresh pot of tea.

'Cheers,' he said. He sat opposite her and drank some of his tea. 'You sure you're okay?'

'Yes,' she said.

'Okay, good. Let's eat then.'

She waited for him to try the food first. She tried the smallest mouthful of some of the sauce. Her stomach made a movement that reminded her to be careful. The tomato was good. She wanted more. But she waited a moment before trying another small mouthful. She could tell he was watching her in a hidden way. She tried the chicken only after he'd finished his entire meal. He went to the kitchen to refill his plate. They always made more than they needed, and they often ate it all in one sitting. She started to eat at the same pace as him. Now that she felt confident, she started to enjoy every small bite. It all felt new.

'I feel so much better,' she said, looking at her empty plate the way a child looks at one of its drawings.

He offered to make some more tea but she insisted on making it. She filled the teapot and said, 'What day is it? Is it Tuesday? It's Tuesday, isn't it?'

He nodded.

'I'll probably go in tomorrow,' she said. 'Who was on the phone earlier?'

'Nobody.'

'I may have been ill, but I wasn't deaf. It was work, wasn't it? You were supposed to have gone in, weren't you? Simon! Did you even tell them you weren't going in? What did you say? What did they say?'

He considered changing the subject, and thought of asking her if she wanted to be a mother. He laughed.

'What?'

'Nothing, I don't know.'

'Really, what?'

'I don't know. Sometimes I laugh for no reason. Really, I don't know what's funny,' he said.

She was suppressing a laugh. 'You're weird, you are.'

'Yeah, you're weird too.'

When he put their plates in the sink, he noticed she hadn't eaten any of the bread. They'd forgotten about it. It didn't matter. It was nice to do something for her that he thought she wanted.

1976: PHOTOGRAPHY

If she'd grown up with a sister she may have enjoyed her company that evening. Sarah's parents had left her alone for the first time. They said they were going to eat somewhere. Her dad only looked like he did when he went to work. The only difference was the absence of a tie. Her mum was wearing a red dress. She had seen photos of her wearing a dress before, but never red. She thought her mum looked pretty but didn't say. It was the last time Sarah saw them together as a couple. They told her again that there was something for her in the fridge. She acted as though they hadn't said anything. They didn't say it a third time. Her mum was in the car waving so she waved back. She waited for the sound of the car engine to start before she closed the front door. She closed her eyes until the engine faded to nothing and walked into the enclosing space of her own silence. She'd never had her own silence. It was always on someone else's terms; a teacher asking a class to be quiet; her father wanting to concentrate on his reading. The quiet house felt bigger and smaller; she thought about this, and then of how to fill her time. She stood in the kitchen and ate the salad her mum had prepared. She believed it would be the final influence her parents would have on her new silence.

She boiled the kettle for a cup of tea. Her dad used to make her tea on Saturday mornings. It tasted better than the one her mum made after school. She tried to make it like her dad made it. He poured the water into the cup a lot quicker than her mum did. Sarah was careful, but made a jolting movement to fill the cup as soon as possible. She stirred the teabag and pushed the teabag hard onto the sides of the cup. Her mum never did this. She only stirred it. Sarah pushed so hard that the cup almost fell from her grip. She carried the tea into the living room, careful not to spill any. She knew how to clear it up and what to use to clear it up, but she still didn't want to spill any tea. A packet of her dad's cigarettes was on the table. He'd be annoyed to find that he's left them. She realised, though, that he could buy another packet in the restaurant, probably. She looked at her dad's cigarettes for a couple of minutes and lit one of her mum's incense sticks, or, as her mum called them, smelly sticks. Her dad called them Indian sticks. Sarah turned the phone off because that's what her mum did when she lit an incense stick. She lit them when she had a bath, but Sarah didn't want a bath. She wanted to sit.

She compared the smoke from the incense to the steam from her tea. The incense was grey and the steam was a thin white. She got up and turned the light off to see if the smoke could still be seen. It couldn't. She turned the light on. She blew the smoke and the steam and their movement was like a wild fox. 'Pang,' her dad would say. She used to laugh when he said that. 'Pang, look at it go.' About foxes, not smoke or steam. She couldn't imagine her father having anything to say about smoke or steam. Sarah focused on keeping her head still until the smoke and steam returned to its calm and upright rising. Spirals weaved around other spirals and Sarah became light headed. She held her head still with her hands. She thought the smoke and steam were running downwards, defying their instructions, going back into the incense stick and into the tea instead of coming from them. She blinked and the order returned. The smoke and steam rose towards the ceiling but falling short of their goal, fading into the silence of the house with her thoughts.

Her dad's newspaper was on the table and its top left corner was in perfect line with the table's corner. She opened it and read the headlines of the articles until stopping at a double spread picture. It was an overturned ferry, pouring slick oil that should have never looked beautiful. But it did. She touched the paper and it was soft. This was the heart of the newspaper. The headlines she had ignored were nothing. All writing was nothing. This picture made her think more than any writing ever did. People may have died but it was so beautiful. This was the word she found herself stuck with: *beautiful.* Every colour was new. The black, in particular, was especially new.

She argued with herself about the idea of black being a colour. She wanted to say that it wasn't, and she was sure she would have done if not for this picture. She drank most of her tea and dunked the lit end of the incense stick into it. It looked like a paintbrush. She stood and turned the light off.

Black.

She tried to walk across the room. She had walked this room countless times, but it was impossible without her sight. It shouldn't be, she thought.

She found the light and stared at the wonder of colour. She turned the light off again, on again, off.

2006: THE PAST AND THE FUTURE

Simon came into the house and took off his coat and shoes. *And when the time was ready, we had to sell the telly*. Sarah put her Bacardi and coke on the side and turned the music down. 'Jess okay?' she said.

'She'll be fine. As soon as your mum starts joking around with her, it'll be here she'll be upset at coming to.'

'She looked a bit down before you took her.'

'Every time we take her anywhere. Honestly, she was fine,' he said.

'Did you tell her we're picking her up in the morning?'

'I said ten, but she'll want to stay longer when the time comes. You'll see.'

'You said that already,' she said.

'Because you keep talking about it.'

'She just looked a little down, that's all.'

He poured a whisky and took a sip. He noticed the coke bottle on the side and added a touch to his whisky. 'We could go to Twins,' he said.

'*Twins* Twins?' she said.

'Why not? You're sounding like it's a bad idea.'

'Bit of a trek.'

'I don't mind. Besides, we haven't been there for years. Would be nice, wouldn't it?'

'I think of that place sometimes,' she said.

'Yeah, let's go then. Come on, we might as well. We've got to do something,' he said.

'Give me half an hour then.'

'I was going to finish this first anyway. There's no rush.'

He finished his drink while reading the lyrics and looking at the artwork of the album sleeve notes. A song he didn't much like came on. He put the album on track one and listened to *Take Me I'm Yours*. When she came downstairs and said she was ready, he looked at his watch. Half past six. He asked her if she was hungry.

'Not one bit,' she said. 'We could get something on our way home, maybe. You're not hungry, are you?'

He wasn't. They left the house after *Cool For Cats*. He hummed it as he drove. They parked at Twins. The old sign looked the same. She didn't know why but, on the way to Twins, she had convinced herself the sign must have changed. They walked inside. He kissed two of his fingertips and planted them on the framed picture of Patti Smith in the entrance.

'You know, I forgot about that,' she said.

'About what?' he said.

'Your obsession with Patti Smith.'

'I can't believe this photo's still here,' he said.

'I can't believe you still have to kiss her.'

'Habit,' he said.

He told her to sit where she wanted and he walked to the bar and ordered a Bacardi and coke and half a lager. He turned around with the drinks and saw her sitting at a table. He walked over.

'When did this place turn special?' he said.

'Special?'

'You know what I mean.'

She did. 'When we stopped coming here, I suppose.'

'Funny, isn't it? How things like that happen.'

'Cheers,' she said. 'For the old times.'

He thought of adding a toast to the future as well, but instead he said, 'Cheers.'

They drank and both commented on feeling old. He told her she still looked about thirty. She didn't believe him and he could tell. He thought of trying to convince her he meant it, but he couldn't think of the best way to do this.

'Hold on,' he said, reaching underneath the table.

'What are you doing?' she said.

'Here,' he said, unfolding a five pound note on their table.

'You found that just now?'

'Sure did.'

'You remember our old rule about money we find, right?'

'What? Share it?' he said.

'No, don't worry. It's not that. But I can't believe you've forgotten.'

'Give me a minute,' he said.

She held a playful shocked expression in place between sips of her drink.

He said, 'Something like use it for something interesting?'

'No, I'll tell you then. The rule was that if we find some money, any amount of money, we have to either spend it right in the moment or give it away.'

'I remember.'

'Because we used to talk about finding thousands of pounds somewhere and having to spend it on something. We used to talk for ages, about what we'd buy for each other and other people.'

'I remember. I can't believe I forgot.'

He ordered more drinks with their winnings: another Bacardi and coke for her and an orange juice for him. The orange juice came in a small glass, one that would normally hold a spirit. As he walked back to the table, he felt people looking at him. He wished he wasn't driving so he could enjoy the place as he used to, warmly influenced, bordering drunkenness. But maybe we'll come here again, he thought. It then occurred to him they would never return. He didn't know why but he knew it.

'You remember why we first came here, don't you?' he said.

'Because Harriet and that hung out here, wasn't it?'

'And now you've forgotten something.'

'Tell me then. Why did we come here then? I'm sure it was Harriet that showed us this place.'

'Who were the first band we saw?' he said.

'The Cocteau Twins, I remember now.'

'And we walked by here together, the day after the concert, and I said we had to go in.'

'After work, wasn't it?' she said.

'I'm not sure. It may have been, but I'm not sure.'

'It was, definitely after work. We were walking home together. You waited for me to finish so we could walk together,' she said.

'If I remember correctly, we saw them on a Saturday so it couldn't have been the day after work,' he said.

'Two days then. We came on a Monday. We used to stay

in bed on Sundays, so we probably first came here on a Monday. That sounds right.'

'So we both forgot something,' he said.

'But I remembered without you telling me. I only had that one little clue. So I'm pretty sure that I win.'

There was a short silence. 'What did we used to talk about? Before Jess,' he said.

'Why? Are you struggling?'

'Of course not; I was just thinking back.'

'We used to talk about music, new albums coming out, films after we'd seen them, we used to go on Thursdays, remember? It was cheaper on Thursdays for some reason. And we talked about anything, everything. Why is your glass so small?' she said.

They laughed.

'We should go to the cinema again. I'd like to,' he said.

'I'd rather buy a DVD. You're forgetting how loud and annoying everyone else can be. We only went all the time to get out, didn't we?'

He made an agreeable noise.

She said, 'Do you feel you need to get out?'

'Not that I need to, not at all. I was only asking if you wanted to go to the cinema.'

'You'd get annoyed with the people talking.'

'All right. I'm an old grumpy man who's forgetting his memories, losing his mind.'

'Want another drink, old man? I'll ask for a bigger glass,' she said, laughing a little.

'Better be off really, get some food. I get grouchy if I don't eat.'

'Okay,' she said.

‘It’s nice how we’ve hung onto this, don’t you think?’

‘Hung onto what?’ she said.

‘This place.’

‘It’s only a pub.’

‘You know what I mean. We’ve kept the same memory, or kept similar thoughts of this place. It’s something that matters, something I’ve thought about before. It’s . . . I don’t know, I’m just happy about it.’

‘Yes, I know what you’re talking about.’

‘Let’s drink up then.’

They finished what was left in their glasses. There was almost nothing in his glass. Raising it to his mouth was more of a gesture than anything. He felt a little strange leaving Twins for what would be, he had decided, the last time.

‘Nice place still, isn’t it?’ he said.

‘Yeah, it’s all right.’

He looked at the sign again. ‘Why don’t we have something inside?’

‘In Twins?’

‘They serve food. Come on,’ he said, already walking towards the entrance again. ‘We rarely buy a meal out. We don’t want to cook tonight. It’s already late. It won’t be much more than a take away.’

‘They never used to serve food.’

‘They do now,’ he said.

‘Okay then.’

They returned to the same table.

‘And maybe we’ll find some more money,’ he said, looking at the floor.

‘Stop that, will you,’ she said.

‘Was only joking.’

'But someone might be looking.'

'How would they know I was looking for money?'

She wanted a pizza, but said she couldn't eat a whole one. He asked if that was all she wanted and she said it was. He went to the bar and ordered one pizza, one salad, and a portion of potato wedges. They said they didn't have wedges so he asked for chips instead. When the food arrived, she said she wouldn't be able to eat it all and he said it didn't matter.

'Shall we get some more chips?' she said after they finished. 'To share though.'

'Okay,' he said, and when a young girl came to collect their empty plates, he ordered another portion. The young girl reached for the tomato sauce and the salt and vinegar, but Simon said, 'We'll need these still.'

'Oh yeah, sorry,' the young girl said. 'You're supposed to order at the bar really, by the way.'

'Should we?' Simon said.

'It's okay. One portion of chips, yeah?' the young girl said.

'Please,' Simon said.

'She's pretty,' Sarah said, when the girl left.

'That's funny. She reminds me of you.'

'How I used to look. That's what you mean.'

'No,' he said.

They ate the chips and Sarah said, 'All right, let's leave. Shall we?'

They stood. He took the car keys from his back pocket, threw them in the air and caught them in the other hand and said, 'Let's.'

She laughed and took his arm. They left Twins and walked to the car. The strange feeling that accompanied him the first time they left Twins, before their meal, was not with him now. He wondered if the meal had made a difference, settled his nerves somehow. A concern came to him: *perhaps it's the drink? The reason I'm calm.* But he told himself it couldn't be. He knew his limits.

'What are you thinking of?' she said.

'I'm thinking of what DVD to buy us for our first cinema night.'

'We could rent. We could join one of those online things. I've got friends who do it. It's not expensive.'

'Online things?'

'I know about them,' she said.

'You don't watch them online though, do you? I don't want to watch films on the computer.'

'No, they send a DVD.'

'Good. We can do that,' he said.

'We'll see if my mum can look after Jess and we'll make snacks and buy a bottle of wine. It'll be so much fun. I can't wait. Really, I can't.'

He changed the gears as seldom as he could. They drove home like that, touching.

II

J AND LAURA

2015: IS IT FINISHED?

Laura hadn't slept. She wondered how he could. What did he mean by *thinking things through*? Why were his eyes so heavy?

'Wake up,' she said.

J opened his eyes.

'I need to know. I hardly slept,' she said.

'Know what?'

Why put me through this? she thought. *Why pretend nothing's wrong?* After a few moments, she replied, 'If you're leaving me. That's what. Are you? Don't make me wait. This hurts. I haven't slept.'

'Why can't you sleep?'

'Just tell me. I'm ready to hear everything, anything.'

'It's okay.'

'What's okay? Tell me what's okay, and tell me what isn't,' she said.

'Things. Us.'

'Us. So we're okay?'

'Yes. What's wrong with you?' he said.

'Are you leaving me?'

'What did I just say? No, I'm not leaving you.' But she

didn't believe him and had known him long enough to trust her instincts. She thought of trying for sleep, but her head was still full of the same thoughts that flickered like a faulty light bulb and kept her from rest last night: He would have done it by now if he wanted to, wouldn't he? But he wants to, doesn't he? What will I do?

'Shall I make us some breakfast? Would you like coffee?' she said.

'Make a pot of tea like normal.'

'Okay,' she said.

'I can make it. Should get up really.'

'No, I'll do it,' she said, leaving the bedroom.

She made a pot of tea, thought of a future alone. She remembered an old friend of theirs who had been alone for years. But their friend had a daughter. She tried to think about something else. But she couldn't. Instead of waiting for him to join her in the kitchen, she took the tea upstairs.

'Would've come down.'

'It's okay,' she said, sitting on the bed.

He sat up to take his tea. She was sure there was no one else. *Did he want to be alone? Who would? Who could?* The wardrobe door was slightly open. She got up to close it and sat again on the bed. She said, 'Tea in bed. Reminds me of our old weekend mornings.'

'Sometimes I thought we'd never get out of bed. Do you remember how cold our first place was?'

'It wasn't just because of the cold, the staying in bed.'

Her tea was too sweet at the bottom where she hadn't stirred it well enough.

'Want another? I'll get them. I'll bring them here?' she said.

'It's okay,' he said. 'Let's go down. I could eat.'

She walked downstairs with their empty cups. She refilled them and sat at the table. He came down ten minutes later. All of her concentration focused on the exact point his slippers met the floor as he walked downstairs and past her into the kitchen. She could hear the impact made by both his slippers onto the carpet and somehow onto the wooden floorboards underneath as well. She heard the two separate sounds at the same time.

'Your tea's here,' she said.

'Okay.'

'We haven't much in. Shall we go out for breakfast?'

'We never go out for breakfast. Where?' he said.

'Just an idea.'

'Where?'

'I don't know. Didn't think of that. It was just an idea,' she said.

'It's okay. We've got enough.'

He toasted some bread and took a jar of marmalade from the cupboard. 'Aren't you having anything?' he said.

'In a bit, I might,' she said.

J took a pencil from the side and started filling in the crossword from yesterday's newspaper. Laura thought of reading. She couldn't remember if she'd recently finished a novel or was halfway through one.

'Shall we go somewhere for the day?' she said, rubbing her eyes.

J looked out of the window and before he replied, Laura said, 'Didn't notice it was raining. But we still can if you feel like it.'

'Not in the rain,' he said. 'Why don't you help me with the crossword?'

She sat with him and they worked it out. J made a pot of tea and noticed it had stopped raining. It still wasn't weather to be in though.

'I can tell you're worried. You don't need to be,' he said.

She held her focus on the completed crossword.

He said, 'You don't need to worry.'

'You said things were okay earlier, I know.'

'Come on. I can tell you're still worried. I can tell something's up.'

'Can you?'

'You're acting differently. The tea this morning, going for breakfast somewhere, wanting to head out in that rain.'

'I often make our first tea, and what's so strange about wanting to drink it in bed?'

'It's not strange. I never said it was. It's different. And there's no problem with difference per se, but there's a reason behind this difference, and it's making me feel guilty. When I see how different you're acting, I feel bad. Because I'm the reason, right? But—and I promise this is true—there's nothing wrong. Listen. There's nothing. Why don't you sleep? I can tell you're tired.'

'Can't sleep.'

He walked into the living room and came back with a DVD box set. He showed her the front cover. She smiled. It was a collection of Mike Leigh films they received a few Christmases ago and hadn't yet got round to watching. He suggested they begin watching it.

'We've been meaning to, haven't we?' she said.

'Come on then,' he said, and they walked into the living room. Before half an hour of *Nuts In May,* she was asleep with her head on his shoulder. He hadn't seen *Nuts In May* for over ten years, possibly longer, and although it was almost precisely as he remembered, the experience was far removed from the first. Instead of laughing aloud, he felt pity for the characters. Laura woke with the running credits.

'Is it finished?' she said.

'You're awake then. Finished just now.'

She took her head from his shoulder.

'We'll have to watch it again sometime. You slept through almost all of it.'

'One day,' she said.

'We could watch another one,' he said, reading the box. '*Another Year, Secrets & Lies* or *Abigail's Party*. They're good ones, aren't they? You liked *Abigail's Party*, didn't you?'

'Don't remember it that well.'

'Don't you?'

'No,' she said.

'*Want another one, darling? Just a little top-up sweetie, all right, there you go.*'

'Oh yeah, I remember. She's good in that, isn't she?'

'Really good. Shall we watch it then?' he said.

'We can watch it. Need a drink though.'

'Which one? *Abigail's Party*?'

'If you like,' she said.

J made the tea. He returned with the full pot and a pint of milk on a tray. 'So we don't have to pause it,' he said.

'Very clever, but you forgot the sugar.'

He brought in the sugar pot.

'I already put sugar in your cup. Ready?' he said, with the remote control in his hand and finger over the play button.

'Before you start it, you said last night you were thinking things through,' she said.

'Did I?'

'You know you did. And please don't pretend you don't remember. I don't mind. I'm not annoyed. I just want you to tell me what it means, what you meant?'

'I don't even remember saying it. Besides, you've said similar things before.'

'We're too old for this now.'

'Too old. You're talking like we're seventy or something.'

'So we're okay? Are we okay?'

'Maybe I thought we weren't when I said it.'

'So you do remember saying it?' she said.

'Maybe I thought we weren't *if* I said it. But I only thought it for a second if I did. Honestly, barely a second. Nothing's going to happen.'

'How comforting,' she said.

'Don't worry.'

'We've been through so much. I don't know what I'd do,' she said, still convinced he was thinking of leaving her. She put her head on his shoulder again and he put his arm around her.

He said, 'I find it a little annoying that you're choosing to believe me then but not now.'

'I can tell when you're telling the truth. There's a difference.'

'What are you talking about?' he said, making every effort to sound as though he had no idea. He reached for the remote and pressed play. After setting the remote on the table, he put his arm around her again. If someone had entered the living room and seen her there, they'd have likely commented on how content the couple looked.

2006: LONG WEEKEND

He hadn't heard her stir and wondered if she had crept out of their bed deliberately quiet to avoid waking him. She probably left the room without looking at him, as if facing him meant facing other things too. She was speaking fewer words to him each day. He tried to think of the last conversation she started. They'd lived separate lives since learning the fact. It defeated their shared aim and made them individual again. But the fact didn't explain everything. It wasn't everything.

He felt the absence of her presence more than he would have felt her actual presence had she woken beside him. Without opening his eyes, he knew she was not there. She was turning into a ghost. He wondered if, when lying in their bed, she impressed upon the pillow at all, creased the sheets. She was as light as a memory. To remember something different, he said the month 'June,' aloud, still with his eyes closed, in an attempt to trigger something from last summer—not that anything particularly memorable happened, but last summer was before winter, before they learned the fact. But nothing happened when he said, 'June.' One syllable accompanied him for a second and then left. His word didn't even sound like a word. It sounded like the noise of a fast car going past. He said it again, deliberately making it sound less like a word. 'Joon.' He noticed the silence in the room. He said, 'July . . . August,' and, though they sounded more like real words to him, still nothing. The silence doubled after each month. He thought about the idea of nothing doubled and doubled again. He thought: if *nothing* could encompass more of the qualities that made it nothing, becoming something more, while at the same time remaining *nothing,* then surely there was no natural end? He thought about getting out of bed, going downstairs, making some breakfast, and doing something. He almost looked forward to Monday morning. There she was, perched at the dining table in the centre of the room, in a shadow cast by nothing.

'Morning,' he said.

'Morning,' she said.

He put the kettle on, made a pot of tea, and poured himself one. He looked over to her, reading the novel she'd been saying she wanted to start for about four months.

'There's tea,' he said.

'I'll get some in a minute, thanks,' she said.

'I can get you one.'

'Just finishing this bit, then I'll get one.'

'You sure?'

She stopped reading and stood. She had to walk around him to get to the teapot. Her shoulder brushed past his arm. He didn't feel anything. She poured her tea.

'You didn't finish the bit you were reading, did you?'

'No,' she said.

'I said I'd make you one.'

'You could've just made it.'

'Right.'

'Don't say *right*. I couldn't concentrate on what I was reading with you talking. I can't even remember the last sentence I read. So I poured it myself.'

'Ri—'

'You know, I fucking hate it when you say *right*. Maybe don't say it.'

He almost said it again without thinking, smiling because he couldn't think of anything else to do.

'I'm not saying you should have made me one, only that you could have. It's not as if you thought I wouldn't want one. When don't I want one?'

A small sound made him turn. Next-door's cat was by the patio window. Last autumn, they let it in to get warm, fed it occasionally, each time admitting they probably shouldn't. He smiled at the cat as if he were smiling to a stranger's baby in a supermarket. He looked back at Laura. 'I think we should start to . . .'

'Start to what?'

He had his answer prepared, but left a little silence to disrupt the rhythm of the coming argument. A slow broken conversation is safer than a sharp one. He sat at the dining table to make his quiet more natural, as if moving to the table and sitting was the distraction that kept him from speaking. 'Nothing,' he said. He closed his jaw tight as he waited to see if his pause had achieved the desired affect. He took a bite out of his toast. It was soft after leaving it for too long. He looked over to the window for the cat but it had gone. He finished the toast and walked over to make more.

'How's the novel?'

'You should know. You've read it,' she said.

'How are *you* finding the novel?'

'Only this far in.'

'Want some toast?'

'No,' she said.

'Okay.'

She looked at the novel's cover as though she was checking for spelling mistakes and said, 'You didn't buy this for me, did you?'

'No. My mum did.'

'We should ask her over soon. Or see her.'

'I see her at least once a week. I saw her last week. I'm seeing her this week too.'

'I said *we* should see her. We could go for a walk—it's getting warmer—or have lunch, or something like that.'

'I could ask her if she's free next weekend.'

'Sure. Ask her,' he said.

'Did you . . .'

'Did I what?'

'Never mind,' he said.

'At least you didn't say *nothing* again.'

The toast popped up. She used this as an excuse to reopen her book and continue reading. He sat at the table again and ate his toast before it turned cold and soft.

'There were more birds this time last year, remember?'

'Not really,' she said, not lifting her head from the novel.

'You don't remember last year or you don't remember the birds?'

She put the novel down, pages spread apart to keep her place. He told her it ruined the spine if it was one of his books, but this one wasn't.

'The birds, of course. Isn't that what you asked me?' she said.

'It's not like we put bread out especially; they were just here.'

'We put bread out.'

'So you do remember?' he said.

'I remember. We put bread out.'

'After they started coming, we did. But they were here before the bread. I wish I knew why.'

'You miss the birds?' she said.

'They may have even been here as early as March last spring.'

'You miss the birds then?'

'I liked listening to them, that's all . . .'

She started reading.

'. . . but not like background music, like they were something to ignore—something one *could* ignore—they were more like company.'

'I know what you're getting at and I don't appreciate it.'

'I'm not getting at that.'

'It's very clumsy, that's all. If you want to speak about it then speak about it. Don't start talking about birds. It's almost pathetic.'

'I was talking about the bloody birds.'

'Okay, okay.'

'Not about that.'

'Okay.'

'If I want to speak about that then I'll just bloody say it.'

'Okay.'

He stood with the intention of leaving the room. Instead, he washed his plate and knife.

'Like another tea?' he said.

‘Thank you.’

He took her cup from the table and poured them both a tea. He sat back at the table.

‘They were nice to listen to. Not boring, but relaxing,’ he said.

‘What’s the most boring thing you can think of? I’m not saying the birds were boring. That’s not why I’m saying this. Just making conversation. I was only thinking. It’s kind of an interesting question, don’t you think? The most boring thing you can think of.’

‘Not sure. I guess you’ve considered it though. Something boring.’

‘Why do you say that?’ she said.

‘Because you brought it up. I’m guessing you have something in mind.’

‘It’s a subject I’ve thought about before.’

‘Well then, what’s the most boring thing you can think of?’ he said.

‘That interview question: *what’s your biggest weakness?*’

‘Yes, and the answers to it. Imagine twenty minutes of listening to that.’

They were both quiet as if thinking of a roll of answers to the interview question, but they were both thinking of the same something else.

‘And we’re going to have to talk about it sometime, you know?’ he said, leaving the room.

When he returned downstairs, she was still reading at the table. The house was quiet except for the ticking of the clock. ‘Could get a paper,’ he said.

‘Do you want one? I don’t mind. Won’t read it.’

‘Might not bother then. You should have some breakfast.’

'I will, but in a while. I don't feel like it right now.'

'Well I'm heading out. I need to, having been at work all week, inside. Want to come or not?'

'Don't be aggressive,' she said.

'Would you like to come with me?'

'Where are you going?'

'For a walk. Walderfield, perhaps.'

'Bit cold for that,' she said.

'It's not too cold.'

'I said a bit cold, not too cold.'

'I'm going to get my things together. If you change your mind, let me know. I won't leave for half an hour yet.'

There wasn't much to do to get ready other than to put on shoes. He sat by the kitchen table and, to keep his mind busy, imagined the table was a desk and that he was wearing a suit, and he waited for the answers to the question—*that I'm a perfectionist . . . that sometimes I get too involved in my work . . . people say I'm a bit serious, maybe . . . a perfectionist . . . that I don't know when to stop working . . . that I work too hard, when I'm told to do something, like instructed by a manager or something . . . too driven for my own good . . . I work hard, too hard? Maybe . . . yeah, a real perfectionist . . . sorry, what was the question? . . . that I'm too honest . . . sometimes my arms go to sleep at the wrist and it's difficult to move them, you know, like when people's feet go to sleep when they sit on them, and I've spoken to the doctor about this, twice; once when I was sixteen after it made me fail an exam because I couldn't write, and another time just recently when I almost ran over this old woman with shopping bags and a small grey dog, but they don't know what it could be, and I can't figure it out, but I guess my wrist thing is a weakness . . . did you ask me something? . . . not coming across well in interviews, selling myself properly . . . did someone just jump out of an upstairs window? I thought I saw a shadow, behind your shoulder, I'm serious, we should check . . . putting my work above my family, priority-wise . . . cancer . . . my constant need to be provided with new and challenging tasks . . . I can't think of one; can I get back to you, before the end of the interview? Perhaps I can email you later today? . . . I get so involved in work that I forget the time and sometimes finish too late, by accident . . . I'm really having trouble with your accent; could you repeat that, please? . . . I tend to exaggerate things, like my memory is slightly flawed or something, like once, when I was very young, I told all my friends I took a six minute piss . . . I can't feign excitement or happiness, even if I want to, you know, my parents knew if they bought me a crappy present for Christmas . . . if you're asking for the truth, man to man, and if you're asking me to be dead honest with you, without the bull, if you pardon the expression, then I'd have to tell you that I'm—*

'Don't think I will come,' she said. 'You don't mind, do you?'

'No, 'course not. Do you remember the time we went to Leeds Castle? It was one of the first real days out we spent together.'

'Why do you bring that up?'

'Do you remember or not?'

'Kind of,' she said.

'It was perfect weather, and I remember feeling so relieved because it had been bloody awful all week. Then when we got there, I realised that, because of the sun, there were loads of people. I couldn't help thinking that I wished it'd been raining. Did I say that at the time?'

'Don't think so. All I remember you going on about was how lucky we were for the sun.'

'It took us ages to park. The line to get in was long. Noisy children with ice creams,' he said.

'I remember.'

'We joined the line behind this family who were talking about their picnic. I think I even remember that they were arguing about whether they packed the sausage rolls or not. Do you remember that they argued for about the whole length of the line?'

'I do now that you say it,' she said.

'I was thinking the whole time *check the picnic box*. That orange ugly box she had. It was making a mark on her arm and must have hurt because she kept moving it up and down her arm. If they'd have checked the box, it would have taken ten seconds, and we wouldn't have had to listen to their bloody arguing anymore. Then we got to the front of the line and we found that the concession price didn't include students. Think it was ten pounds each.'

'What are you getting at?'

'Don't know, remembering. We left the castle after maybe forty minutes, and ten minutes of that was probably because of walking slowly behind slow families. Because of the entrance fee, we didn't have much money so we bought a baguette and some cheese and sat in the park outside the castle: a park that costs nothing to enter. We sat in the sun, ate our lunch, and looked up at the thin castle windows. I think we even counted them. You leaned into me and we sat there for hours. I think you slept,' he said.

'Are you saying you want me to come with you today?'

'I always want you with me. Who wants to be alone? But

that's not what I'm saying. I was just remembering, aloud. I wanted you to know what I was thinking, and I wanted there to be some noise in the house. Too much quiet makes me uncomfortable. You know that.'

He wanted something to say before leaving, a sentence more filling than *goodbye*.

She said, 'By the time you come back, I'll have something for you, I promise.'

'Looking forward to it.'

'You off then?'

He moved towards the door and said, 'How can we talk about something that doesn't exist?'

'Some-*thing*?'

'Yes, I'm off,' he said. 'Goodbye.'

'Hold on. You could get a paper,' she said.

'Okay. See you later then.'

'Goodbye.'

With the sound of the closing door, he remembered exactly why the silence of the house bothered him the way it did. It reminded him of winter; the two months of waking at three am. After a few nights of attempting and failing to return to sleep, he started walking downstairs upon waking. Giving up and sitting in the cold kitchen, too distracted or too tired to read, never hungry, the only colour a dry washed out night-grey, the only light the little oven lights, only two or three sounds, the faint rustling of hidden foxes, the ticking of the clock, his heartbeat like footsteps. His head elsewhere in those small hours; hours that were long as they were cold, and as still as they were quiet. After a certain amount of time, he often felt that it would have been a good time to paint. But he wasn't a painter. Or it would have been a good time to run if he felt like exercising. Placing painting alongside running made him realise he knew nothing about what it was to be an artist. Did an artist need energy and to be fed and full to create? He didn't know. He knew what it meant to be able to run or play a sport, but he didn't know what it meant to make anything.

He avoided a table seat on the train so nobody could sit opposite, and he looked out of the window, counting shades of colour, without thinking. He left the train, sat on the platform, and watched the sky for birds through the darkening grey. None were visible. The day could have gone either way. He left the station, choosing the long walk to the riverfront, through the small town beforehand. He walked the thin and steep road up to the graveyard. The whole village could be seen from there. He picked out the two or three new buildings since his last visit. This felt like a dramatic change before he remembered he hadn't visited for a few years, perhaps even five. Thankfully, the village remained in an almost perfect circle. The river wound around it before shooting west, shaped like a ring on a piece of string. At sunset, if lined up right, the whole stretch of the river glowed. He traced the river until he could no longer see it. On a clear day, the bird nests could be seen in the trees that lined the river, but it was not clear. He looked to the nearby gravestones. His dad once told him of a great auntie being buried there, but he didn't remember her name or where in the graveyard she rested. He could have phoned and asked someone, but it wasn't important. Having read three headstones, he completed the row, feeling he should. His grandmother's funeral came to him. Halfway through the service, he looked around and counted all of the people in the church who would have never been born if not for her, or if not for a number of small and seemingly insignificant decisions which she, or someone she knew, once made. Twenty-two people. He walked away from the graveyard, after almost entering but choosing not to enter the church for a quick look inside.

He walked through the village with his head bowed, trying to remember why he didn't head straight to the riverfront. The eventual sight of the water, however, failed to satisfy. He took a few deep breaths and walked alongside his flattened expectations. The tide drew breath and he caught a glimpse of a thin beach. The temptation to walk on the sand came but went with a sharp breeze that stung his ears. He stood his collar to prevent earache. Two fishermen nodded to him. J had thought fishing was prohibited here but he wasn't sure. He nodded back. A lady with her dog walked by. She said hello to him. He nodded to her. A man and his boy sat on a bench, facing the water. The boy was flicking through a pack of football stickers at great speed as his dad looked over his boy's shoulder. Every now and then one spoke or pointed. The shine from the water made J look away. Two birds took flight from two branches. He would have continued walking but the river winded right, cornering him. It must have looked like a hook from above. Without being willing to get a little wet, there was nothing to do except turn back. And once turning back, there was nothing to do but return home.

'I've been calling,' Laura said, before the front door closed.

'Didn't take my phone.'

She looked as if she would be angry if not so tired. 'We need to talk.' Her voice was low and even.

'I know. I've been wanting to for . . .'

'Not about that. Something else. You should call Si.'

‘Sarah’s Simon?’

‘God, yes, Sarah’s Simon. You should call him. He called earlier.’

‘About what?’

‘Call him. I shouldn’t say.’

‘Why?’

‘I don’t know,’ she said.

‘Tell me.’

‘Don’t make me.’

‘Tell me, Laura. This isn’t fair.’

‘Sarah’s dead. He was driving. Just call him, please.’

‘What?’

She walked away to give him the space to understand.

‘When?’ he said.

‘Last night. Please call him,’ she said. ‘I told him I’d tell you to.’

‘And I’m supposed to what? Christ, what will I say? What did you say? I can’t believe this. What did you say? Jess, is she okay?’

‘I don’t know,’ she said.

‘Was she in the car?’

‘No, no, no. She’s safe. I know that. But I don’t know if she knows yet. That’s what I thought you meant. She’s at Sarah’s mum’s. She was there last night, before it happened, when it happened. So she might not know. She’s only nine. I don’t know if she knows. I don’t know if she’d understand. How do you tell a nine year old her mum’s gone?’

He started to leave the room but stopped. ‘What did you say then? Tell me,’ he said.

‘I can’t remember what I said. I don’t think I said anything. Just that I’d tell you to call. He asked me to. He’s waiting.’

'I'm positive it's the last thing he's thinking of.'

He continued looking at her, knowing she had something to say. 'Yes,' he said.

'It might be on his mind. Remember after we found out our thing? Remember I wanted to call my dad? I felt like I couldn't think until everyone I had to tell had been told. I told Si I could tell you—I offered to—but he said he wanted to.'

'So now I have to pretend to not know on top of everything else?'

'No. He won't care. I don't know. Call him soon, please.'

He took the phone and walked upstairs. He returned a few moments later. 'No answer,' he said.

'Call his mobile. Did you call his mobile?'

'No. Why didn't you say that before?'

'Call his mobile.'

He walked upstairs again.

'And don't take it out on me,' she said to herself. She started to cry and walk around the room.

J came downstairs. 'Didn't realise he was in hospital.'

Laura stood. Her hands were on her stomach. 'Not serious though, is he? He said it wasn't serious when I spoke to him. It's not, is it?'

'No.'

He walked over to her and sat. She sat too. 'Did he ask you about Jess, about us taking care of her?' he said.

'No. Did he ask you then?'

'He's going to see how Sarah's mum is, but he wanted a back up, just in case.'

'He could have asked me earlier,' she said.

'It doesn't matter, does it? But that's why he wanted to speak to me. He'll be taking care of Jess anyway. I think he's worried, looking for security.'

'It's terrible. I can't think. It's been like this all day. I tried to call you, but I couldn't get through. It's felt like a horrible secret. I thought once I'd told you I'd start thinking again, but I can't.'

'I can't think either. Couldn't even talk to him properly. I didn't,' he said.

'I'm sure you did. You're his friend.'

'I called him *Simon*,' he said.

'You were nervous, that's all. You don't always call him Si anyway. I've heard you call him Simon before.'

'Not to him, I don't think so. It's Si to his face and Simon the rest of the time. It always has been.'

'It's nothing compared to what I did,' she said.

'What did you do?'

'I made him tell me again. Imagine how difficult it was for him. And I made him tell me again.'

'How? What did you say? What do you mean?'

'He told me and I said: *she isn't*. That's all I said. Can you believe it? And then there was this terrible silence, which he spoke over by telling me what he'd already told me.'

'It's a normal reaction,' he said, not sounding like himself.

'Did he tell you how it happened?'

'Of course he told me.'

'I'm so tired. I can't believe what's happened.'

'So unlucky,' he said.

'He barely had time to take the key out when it came. If they'd had a driveway she'd still be alive.'

'How the fuck can someone hit them there? Probably a drunk,' he said, standing.

'You don't know that. Please relax, sit here again,' she said.

He was looking out of the window.

'J,' she said. 'Sit next to me. Please.'

It felt disrespectful to listen to music or watch television. They couldn't think of anything to do but cook.

They sat to eat.

J said, 'This is the worst Saturday of my life. I feel like I've been sat in front of a horrible film that I'm not allowed to look away from. All day's been like this. I knew it from the moment I woke and you weren't there.'

'I was there.'

'Not when I woke, in the bed. You were down here.'

'I'm not always in bed when you wake,' she said.

'I know. But any other time, I'd put the radio on. I didn't feel like it this morning. Something was up. I knew it. And then I didn't pour you a tea, but normally I . . .'

'I seriously don't care about that right now. I didn't mean to make such a big thing of it.'

They tried to eat. After forty minutes, he'd finished his and she'd managed half. 'The tea, this morning. I know you don't care, but I didn't make you one because I couldn't make my mind up whether you wanted one or not. I couldn't think. I can't think. We haven't spoken properly since . . . you know. Have you spoken to anyone? I know you told your dad. How much did you tell him?'

'I only told him the thing, and nothing else. I couldn't. Nothing else than what we know. You know what he's like anyway. He wouldn't want to talk about that for long. What dad would? He was good about it though.'

'Anyone else?' he said. 'Sorry, that's none of my business.'

'No, it isn't.'

'But we need to talk. I don't know how we can think of anything else before we do. I can't think of Sarah and Simon until we do. I can't even listen to the radio until we do.'

'I understand, but we need to think of Sarah and Simon and Jess. This isn't me putting things off, and this isn't me being awkward, you know, deliberately awkward. You understand, don't you?'

'You're right,' he said.

'Come here.'

He rested his head where she'd invited him. They sat like that for a while before going upstairs. It was dark but neither of them knew the time. He said, 'When did we last have them over?'

'The sixth of last month.'

'That was quick.'

'I was thinking about it earlier on. I made lasagne. You made your flan. You wore a shirt, your blue one.'

'Tell me more about it.'

'Your shirt?' she said, laughing. She soon stopped herself laughing and apologised.

'Don't say sorry. Tell me more about the evening,' he said.

'They were late. Fifteen minutes, I think. Maybe more. You were annoyed, of course. Sarah wore those long earrings. The only other time I remember her in earrings were her wedding pictures and that anniversary party, God, remember that? She looked nice when she came over. Simon had this old hooded coat on, which he didn't take off until after we sat down to eat. He forgot to, I think. You asked us all if we fancied a coffee. You said you did. But none of us felt like one so you never made one, not even for yourself. You got a bit annoyed when all three of us tried to convince you to make yourself one. I noticed and stopped. But those two insisted you make yourself one. Simon even said he'd have one if that changed anything. Then I smiled at you and you stopped looking annoyed. You changed the subject. I wish I could remember what you changed it to. You put some bread in the oven and then we had it with olives, olive oil, pate. Simon tore the bread with his hands every time he wanted some. I watched you wait until either me or Sarah took the next bit before you had more. I was worried Simon noticed, but I don't think he did. Sarah looked so beautiful.'

Laura covered her mouth with her hand.

'You don't have to carry on. I know it's difficult,' he said.

'It's okay. Just give me a minute.'

She walked out. When she came back, her eyes were still wet, but she was smiling.

'Did I tell you how I got to know her?' she said.

'At school. You were both teachers,' he said.

'*How* I got to know her, not where.'

'I can't remember. Tell me.'

'Maybe I haven't told you. I knew her, of course, but I hadn't spoken to her that much in my first few months. I'd hardly spoken to anyone. I was doing that assembly. Do you remember, the one I was so worried about a few months after starting? Everything I'd planned for the assembly had finished and there were about seven minutes left. I didn't know what to say. I felt myself blushing and I stood there like I was lost or something, my class behind me, silent as toys. I was praying one of them to play up just so I'd be able to fill some time asking them to behave. If the head teacher was there I might have told her I was finished, but she wasn't there. All the other teachers were equals so I felt I couldn't ask them. It was like

I was in charge. Well, I was in charge, wasn't I? But I couldn't say anything. Seven minutes is a long time. Then Sarah put her hand up and said: *Mrs Roberts, I've remembered something. Would it be okay to butt in and say something? You have finished, haven't you?* And I said: *Okay Mrs Caldwell, that's fine*. And she smiled to me and started talking about next month's parents evening, and then about the Christmas play, and then, I think, about one of the sports teams, the football team, I think. They had a match that evening. Anyway, it was clear she was making it up to fill in the time. I loved her for that. So we became friends.'

'You never told me that. She really was such a nice person. *Was*. How weird and how wrong does that sound?'

'And they were so nice about our cooking. Do you remember that? After the flan, I told them that I made the lasagne and you made the flan, and then I asked them which they preferred. They wouldn't say. They were so polite.'

J thought she was going to cry again, but she continued speaking after a short pause. 'She was so nice to me when I told her about our thing. But not like other people were. She really meant it. She meant it like it was her pain. There was no trying. It was there as though it had always been there. I could see it.'

'Didn't realise you told her.'

'I had to talk to someone.'

'You're saying I wouldn't have, aren't you?'

'I don't know,' she said.

'Because I tried and I wanted to.'

'Maybe I didn't want to talk to you about it. I don't know. I'm fed up of it. Of thinking about it,' she said, letting her mind drift somewhere else. She thought of Simon and what

Sarah used to tell her about him. Sarah used to worry he didn't have any hobbies and never seemed like other people. She said he looked lost. Sarah felt the pressure of being everything to him. Laura was close to asking J what Simon did in his spare time.

J said, 'I forgot how much like fear this is.'

'What do you mean?'

'Grieving. It's exactly like being scared.'

'Suppose it is in a way,' she said.

'Its association with death makes you think it would be all numb and still, but there's nothing still about it.'

'No,' she said.

'We should do something tomorrow. I don't know what, and we'll decide tomorrow, but we should.'

'Okay.'

'You must feel as though you need to get out,' he said.

'What did I say? I said okay.'

'J,' she called, from what he thought was sleep.

'I'm awake. What is it? What's wrong?'

Some light was coming through the curtain. He watched as her eyes lost focus. 'What is it?'

'Nothing. Good morning. It was nothing,' she said.

'It must be something. What were you thinking?'

'I don't want to say,' she said.

'Please tell me. Was it a dream?'

'Yes.'

'You can tell me.'

'I dreamt of Sarah. She phoned to tell me it was all a mistake. She hadn't died. It felt real. Thought it was. She said she knew everyone was upset and I should tell them she's fine.

I thought it was real. I think I was going to tell you she was okay, that she was alive. But seeing your face changed that. I remembered it all. And I almost hate you for making me remember that she really is dead. It doesn't make sense.'

'I've dreamt similar things before,' he said. 'I know it's horrible.'

'I wonder how long it would have taken me to realise if I were alone.'

'Not long,' he said.

'Can't believe all this, really.' She covered most of her face with a blanket. He rested his head on her shoulder, suppressing tears.

He said, 'Do you want to go out today?'

'What else would we do?'

'Maybe it would do us good.'

'I think so,' she said.

When they were downstairs, they both felt a little better. He had breakfast. She didn't.They sat in the car. He turned the engine on, then off.

'I don't know what I'd do if it happened to us,' he said.

'If what happened?'

'Anything. I can't drive. I don't want to. Not today.'

'Do you want me to?'

'I *need* you to. I told you, I mean it, I can't.'

They swapped seats.

'You're sure it's still okay that I drive? It's not that you want both of us to not drive, is it?' she said.

'I'm fine with you driving. Let's go.'

She drove them to a point on the coast between two semi-popular places. On only two or three occasions had their visit to this point been shared with any other visitors, and their company was only ever passing, people walking the six miles from one destination to the other. Due to the time of year, they were sure to be alone. She parked facing the sea, on the grass, close to the cliff-edge. There was no one to tell them to not.

'Make sure I'm in reverse before we leave,' she said.

'Was that a joke?'

'I don't know. You want lunch now? I know I do.'

'Only had breakfast an hour ago. Told you that you should've had breakfast,' he said.

'But we've got food here, now. Forget it then.'

'Okay, sorry. I'll have something,' he said, stretching to the back seat for the food.

'I can wait,' she said.

'You're hungry. Let's have something. Want the tea as well?'

She nodded so he reached for the flask.

'So many seagulls,' she said.

He took half a sandwich and asked her if she wanted the other half. They ate most of what they had packed and left the car for a short walk. The tide was in so they kept to the cliff-top.

'Really don't think I'll ever know a more perfect couple, a more perfect family,' she said.

'It isn't too late. You never know.'

'I don't know.'

'There are other ways,' he said.

Almost by instinct, and because it was the natural next beat of the conversation, she wanted to ask him what those *other ways* might be, but she stopped herself; he didn't know what he meant, not exactly. They would only be speaking about vague ideas if they continued. It would have nothing to do with them, not yet. It would be like talking about the person you would have been if you weren't yourself. There's no point.

She would see if he wanted to drive the car home, when it was time. It was something that was better getting over sooner rather than later.

1991: HOW I DECIDE

So this is how I decide, he thought. J was almost glad. The decision was out of his hands. Laura or Rebecca had become Rebecca. He had been expecting one to find out about the other, every time Laura said they needed to talk, and every time Rebecca refused to explain a new bad mood, so at least that wouldn't happen now. J and Rebecca were outside. Their taxi was late.

'Nervous?' he said. 'I'm nervous too.'

'Who said I was? I'm not.'

He looked back at the campus. He caught the reflection of her crossed arms in a window. Even with her back turned, he could tell. He had spent twenty pounds on the coat he was wearing. Too late to return, he thought. He turned from the window and looked down the road. She was looking at her feet. He was sure they were the only two on campus not drinking or laughing. The taxi came and the driver asked where they were going. Rebecca said, 'NHS walk-in centre,' speaking slowly, simplifying each syllable. J didn't hear what the driver said. He only knows he said something because Rebecca spoke again. 'No, thank you.'

J was wondering how to look upon hearing the news, and how to make a choice. She turned to J and said, loud enough so that the driver could hear, 'You told them on the phone. I heard you tell them where.'

'Not embarrassed, are you?' J said.

'Will you listen to yourself?'

The tone of her voice was telling. He hoped he was wrong, but he was sure she had already made up her mind.

'We should . . .' he said and stopped himself because he remembered that nothing yet had been confirmed.

'Should what?'

'Forgot what I was going to say,' he said.

'You said *we should*, then you stopped.'

'I know. I forgot.'

'Right,' she said.

But although he stopped himself saying it, he couldn't stop himself thinking about it. He would tell her he was willing to leave university and get a job, and this might change her mind. It would at least make a difference, wouldn't it? But her mind was made up, wasn't it? But they didn't even know yet anyway. How could she have already decided? The journey was short. They walked in together but he sensed that she didn't want him to follow. He stopped short and walked around the waiting room with his hands in his pockets, watching her at reception. It looked as though she was speaking to the point. Her facial features moved closer to the centre of her face at each question. She wrote something, or signed something, and took a seat. He joined her.

'We have to wait a bit,' she said.

'Of course.'

'Of course?'

'Can't expect to walk straight in, can we?'

'Told you we should have booked,' she said.

'You can't book in. There are no appointments at a walk-in centre.'

'You're sure of that, are you?'

'Won't be a long wait anyway,' he said.

'So you're not sure?'

'Pretty sure. Why are we talking about this?'

After a short period of silence, he asked about university. They spoke about an assignment she had to write by next week. J stood with her when someone called her name. She afforded the person who came through to call her name a smile. They had already agreed she would go in alone. He didn't mind and made it clear to her he still didn't. When she walked away, he went outside. If he'd had cigarettes, he would have smoked one. He watched through the glass in case she came out early. His face would appear in the reflection and he would get lost in a thought until he remembered to look for her again. He returned inside within ten minutes and sat where he could see her return. His hands were cold.

A doctor walked with her. She looked at J and she smiled. The doctor waved her goodbye, smiling. She walked to J and said, 'I'm not,' while planting her hands on his stomach and guiding him towards the exit.

'Wow, okay,' he said.

'Good, right?'

'Of course.'

'We can walk back. I know where we are,' she said.

'I don't,' he said.

'You don't want to walk?'

'I don't mind walking.'

‘Then what were you saying *I don’t* to?’

‘I don’t know where we are,’ he said.

‘You don’t live here, do you? If we were in your town, I wouldn’t know where I’d be, most likely. It’s a nice evening to walk. Remember London? We walked everywhere.’

‘We were only there a few days,’ he said.

‘But we walked all the time. I loved it.’

‘You’ve cheered up,’ he said.

‘Wonder why that is. Don’t be weird, Angel.’

They walked back to campus. It took only half an hour. The taxi was a waste of money. He thought of starting a conversation as they walked home but didn’t.

‘Sit there,’ she said, when they entered her bedroom.

He sat on the edge of her bed. She looked through three shopping bags on her desk. He almost started speaking, but he wasn’t sure how to begin. He still had his coat on.

‘You need to tell me what you like. I’m not keeping everything,’ she said.

She stripped to her underwear and took a little time to choose the first item. He wanted to talk. This was typical. He couldn’t think of one occasion they’d spoken about anything on his terms. Of course, there probably were such times, but he couldn’t think of any in this moment. He was starting to think about something important. She turned her naked back to him and bent forward, teasing a pair of tight jeans up her legs. The jeans had a rip across one thigh and a pattern not unlike a tribal tattoo across the other. They stopped at the knee. She was still only wearing a bra on her top half. She walked a couple of steps closer. Perhaps she wanted him to pull her to the bed. He could have reached. He didn’t know if she wanted him to pull her closer or not. He wanted to talk.

'I'm not sure about them either,' she said.
'I didn't say anything.'
'I can tell. Even your silence is helpful, Angel.'
'Really?' he said.
'I'd know if you liked them. I know you.'
'Do you?'
She removed the jeans. He hardly noticed her nakedness beneath his desire to talk and the important thought he was holding. She was in her second outfit and looking to him for approval. She looked younger.
'Very nice,' he said.
If she weren't as good looking, the outfit wouldn't have worked. The trousers were a faded brown and he could imagine someone wearing them for a job interview. She had a long green cardigan over a loose fitted t-shirt and he couldn't believe the outfit worked. Perhaps it only worked because it made people notice her pretty face over what she was wearing.
'You really like it?' she said.
'I do. It makes you look more intellectual,' he said. This was a misstep. He realised as soon as he said it.
'Thanks,' she said and undressed. There was no use correcting himself. He had said it.
He knew they wouldn't get around to talking about what he wanted to talk about. They'd either get into bed together and have sex or spend an hour talking about why he didn't think she looked intellectual. And he thought again of what he wanted to talk about. He was going to tell her about how he felt when he thought she was pregnant. He was going to tell her that he didn't mind and that he could imagine spending his life with her. He was going to say, without actually saying it, that he had chosen her over Laura. It was already ridiculous.

The third item was a thin summer dress. She smiled, taking it out the bag, handling it as though she was frightened it could easily be torn. 'Can already tell you're keeping this one,' he said.

'Definitely. Still want to show you though. Isn't it pretty?'

The dress was mostly white, but speckled with small flower designs; red poppies, it looked like, and yellow daisies.

'It's pretty. You'll have to wait a little while though,' he said. It was February. He wondered why they were even selling summer dresses already.

'I know, but I can wait.'

'Put it on then,' he said.

She lifted it above her head and it fell onto her body effortlessly. It wore close to her breasts and stomach and showed off her figure. The edges of the dress were frayed, which was about the only thing preventing it from looking like a young child's dress.

'Isn't it cute, Angel?' she said.

'Very.'

His decision came almost by itself. It was only when he caught himself wondering how to do it that he first realised he had already made the decision. Laura. He was so nervous that he began to question whether it was the right decision. But it was. He would do it that night. He had to.

'You'll look really nice in summer, in that dress,' he said, knowing he wouldn't see Rebecca in her dress that summer, or even out of this dark little room. He would at least wait until she removes the dress and puts it away. He thought of her wearing the dress in summer. The last thing he wanted was for the dress to remind her of him, tonight. It was the least he could do. He wondered how he would get home, it being late, cold.

1992: CAN YOU STILL SEE A LIGHT?

Laura rested her hand on his chest; when she couldn't sleep, she concentrated on how his chest rose and fell with his breathing. She liked a house to make its own noise, and it sometimes helped her sleep, but she couldn't hear any natural sounds. J's housemate was playing music. It travelled through the walls, covering any natural sounds that might have been there, and came to them stripped of meaning, dull bass tones.

'Can't sleep either,' he said.

She made a quiet noise.

'You can sleep tomorrow. You've no lectures,' he said.

She wondered if she should let him rest. He had to be up at ten.

'Take your shirt off,' she said.

'Why?'

'Because I said.'

'I just put it on . . . but okay.'

'That's better,' she said.

'Don't I smell?'

'Yes, but I like the way you smell.'

'Really?' he said.

'When I'm the reason, of course I like it.'

The curtains weren't closed tightly enough. She could make out a few lights from the house opposite theirs. There was the light from a lamppost too, placed almost directly outside their window, but that never bothered them; they were used to it. The lights from other people's houses bothered her though.

'I want to close the curtains, but I really don't want to get out of bed. I'm too comfortable,' she said.

'Too lazy. I'll do it.'

'But you're why I'm comfortable. You're the reason I feel all lazy and nice. I don't want you to go either.'

'Then try to concentrate on something else.'

'I'm trying. I've been trying,' she said.

'I think you should let me fix the curtains. You know it'll only bother you more.'

'Okay.'

He left the bed, careful to keep her covered with the sheets. He wondered if she noticed things like this. He fixed the curtains. 'Is it okay now?' he said.

'You look nice,' she said, with a smile. It was too dark to see, but obviously there.

'Is it okay?' he said, wishing she would answer so he could return to the warm sheets.

'You should take your shorts off.'

He laughed and said, 'I think it's okay. The curtain's fixed. You won't see any lights.'

'Well?' she said.

'What?' he said.

'Your shorts. You should take them off.'

'Okay,' but he only removed them after rejoining her in

bed. She moved beside him, trying to find the comfortable spot again. When she stopped moving, he closed his eyes.

'I was thinking about my parents,' he said. 'They should have done more.'

'More for you?'

'For themselves. The time went so quickly.'

'You're speaking like they're dead.'

'I'm not trying to. It's the last thing I want to think about. But they are old. You can't say they're not. And they got old so fast,' he said, his eyes still closed. 'I swear they didn't age, or I didn't notice them age, as I was growing up, but these last few years, I've really noticed it.'

'How?' she said.

'I don't know. Both sets of neighbours died. Actually, one of the four is alive. One moved to a home after her husband died. Anyway, both houses were empty all of a sudden. That was the biggest thing. A young couple moved in on one side—into John and Hilda's, I think you met them, didn't you—and the other house is up for sale, which makes it look like a young house again and, all of a sudden, my parents are the old neighbours. And dad turned sixty, mum stopped dying her hair, I don't know.'

'Don't be sad,' she said.

'I'm not sad, exactly, not for them anyway. It's only natural, isn't it?'

'What is it then?'

'Maybe it's worry,' he said.

She closed her eyes and concentrated on his breathing, all of her thoughts in one place. She would have been asleep in minutes had he not spoken again.

'There's so much I want us to do,' he said.

'There's a light still.'

'No there isn't . . . are you sleeping?'

'Sorry?' she said.

'Are you sleeping?'

'Almost. Okay?'

'I was talking to you and you said something in your sleep.'

She rose.

'You don't have to,' he said.

'Hot chocolate?' she said, with a tired smile.

'You're saying that because I can't sleep. You shouldn't have to stay up too. It's okay, honestly. You can sleep. I'll stop talking. I know it's annoying. I'll stop.'

'It's okay. I want to stay up with you. But you have to make the hot chocolate. That's the only condition.'

'Okay,' he said.

He walked through to the cold kitchen. There was something distant and intangible in the quiet. It felt like waiting. It crossed his mind that this dread may have come entirely from himself. He was looking at his housemate's plates in the sink and wondering why he was still leaving them to soak overnight. He dismissed his thoughts of the quiet and the plates and pictured Laura instead. He made the hot chocolates, put marshmallows and chocolate shavings on hers, and took them into the room. It was difficult to open the door so he opened it noisily. He apologised as he walked in, though there was no need.

'Yummy,' she said.

'Would you like ice cream as well?'

She smiled.

'Okay, I'll get some,' he said.

He returned with the ice cream. She was sitting with her

naked legs on show. They were like light. He moved the coffee table closer to the bed so they could rest their midnight picnic on it. He took the duvet and covered them both. She took a sip.

'Is it okay?'

'It's perfect. Better than the one you made last week,' she said and laughed. Remembering, he laughed too.

She kissed his cheek and told him she liked it when he didn't shave.

'Did you know there's no clock in the kitchen?' he said.

'Were you talking about your parents earlier?'

'I mentioned them, but I wasn't talking *about* them; it was about me, and maybe about us. But I don't know exactly. It's okay. This is okay, sitting with you.'

'Just okay?'

'More than okay.'

'But you're not tired?' she said.

'I'm not, but I don't need to be.'

She put her hand on the wall.

'What are you doing?'

'Don't know,' she said. 'I like the feeling of this wallpaper. Have I told you that?'

'No.'

'Are you sure?'

'I think I'd remember something like that,' he said.

'Why? It's not weird, is it, liking the feel of something?'

'Guess not.'

She ate some ice cream and finished her hot chocolate, using the ice cream spoon for the marshmallows at the bottom of her cup. The dull bass tones finished beating.

'That's your favourite part, isn't it?' he said.

'How can you tell? Next time you can add more marshmallows if you want.'

'Okay, I will.'

'So what are you thinking about?'

'Right now?'

'Right now.'

'About your legs, how good they look, even in the dark.'

She smiled, felt surprise. She looked at her legs and kicked them in a swinging motion from the bed as if she was in water and trying to keep afloat. 'They're too short,' she said.

'No they're not. They're perfect, really. And then I started thinking that I wanted us to go somewhere, do something.'

She ate some more ice cream and handed him the tub to finish it, which he did. She stopped kicking and slumped onto the bed. He joined her. He kissed the centre of her chest and wished they hadn't finished the ice cream.

'Where are you taking me then?' she said.

'Where would you like to go?'

'South America, Brazil. I want us to dance in Brazil. Think that sounds good?'

'I do.'

'But maybe my legs are too short and too white to dance in Brazil, with all those long tanned legs around. I'd look silly. I'd feel silly.'

'I hope you're joking.'

'Half joking,' she said.

'Anywhere else?'

'Barcelona. Everyone talks about Barcelona, don't they? It feels like everyone else has been there, and everyone falls in love with it. Do you really like my legs?'

'I love your legs. Where first then? Brazil or Spain?'

'Brazil.'

'That would be my choice as well,' he said.

She moved her head to his shoulder and kissed his neck.

He said, 'What about other things? Where would you want us to live? What kind of life do you imagine?'

She didn't know why, but she didn't want to talk about it. Still, she answered. 'I feel like I want noise. It's what I imagine when I think of the future. Like living in a big city. Always music, places to go. Then a big family, one day. It would never be quiet, except for the small hours when we want to stay up all night, like this, having sex and midnight picnics.'

'Sounds good.'

'So you like my plan? You don't think it's too obvious?'

'What do you mean obvious?' he said.

'Don't you think everyone wants to go to those places, and then have a big family? It's hardly unique, is it?'

'But it will be,' he said, not knowing what he meant.

'Are you sure it's perfect? My plan?'

'Why not?'

He looked at the time. He took the cups and the ice cream through to the kitchen. She watched him get out of bed and walk out, still naked. He came back into the bedroom ten minutes later. She was awake.

'You're so cold,' she said.

He looked tired. She tried to relax, but couldn't.

'I don't know what I want,' she said.

'I know,' he said.

'You kept asking me, but I really don't know. We don't need to know, do we? Not yet.'

'Probably not.'

'Exactly. We'll probably only change our minds anyway,

won't we?' she said, lifting her head an inch from his shoulder.

'Probably.'

'Do you know what *you* want?' she said.

'I guess not,' he said.

Resting her head on the pillow, she said, 'And that's why you can't sleep.'

'That's why I can't sleep.'

Her face was turned to the window. She saw the playful shadow of a pouncing cat. If there was a mouse outside, Laura couldn't see it. She loved the idea of a cat chasing a mouse. When she was seven, she found a mouse running across the living room. She told her dad to set their cat on it. But when she saw the dead mouse, she cried. She told her dad she would be sick if he didn't take it away. Still, later that afternoon, she watched the same spot to see if she could find another mouse for her cat to play with, tear apart. He arched his head to see if she was asleep; she'd been still for a while. Her eyes were open.

'What's wrong?' he said.

'Nothing.'

'Can you still see a light?'

2004: SPARE TIME

J and Laura were walking through the park and she said they should get coffee. They ordered and sat on the balcony, overlooking part of the park. J was watching a father and daughter.

'Want to swap?' she said.

'Yes.'

So she moved to the shade and he sat in the sun. The waiter brought over their coffees. He knocked J's cup and J could see that the handle looked sticky with coffee. J made a point of cleaning the cup with a napkin as the waiter stood by their table. The waiter said nothing and walked away. Laura looked at J and he smiled back.

'Gorgeous, isn't it?' he said.

They drank their coffees. He wanted another one, but he didn't want to turn around to get the waiter's attention. He asked Laura to order, but she didn't want to stand either.

'He'll be over soon. You're so impatient. Give it time,' she said.

'What?'

The sun went in and he shivered.

'You can't be cold,' she said.

'I'm not.'

'Why did you shiver then?'

'I don't know. I just did,' he said.

They sat for five minutes or so, without saying anything.

'Look how she walks,' he said, and they watched the woman walk from the edge of the park to the town hall, about fifty steps, maybe more.

He was looking for the bench they sat at earlier that summer. They decided it was the best bench in the park, or the bench with the best view. Someone on the bench could see the fountain and still hear the water over the children playing in the other side of the park; someone on that bench could see two different statues and a small birds nest on a branch in the closest tree. After they saw the nest, they saw three more on separate branches on the same tree. When they finally got up from the bench, they looked at the other trees. Some of them had one nest on their branches, but none had more than one.

'Fancy chicken later?' she said.

'Don't mind,' he said.

'What's wrong?'

'Hardly matters, does it?'

The waiter came, catching J in mid-thought. They ordered another coffee and J convinced himself that what he was thinking of couldn't have been important because he couldn't remember what it was. The father kicked a football to his girl. The coffee came.

'Such a nice day,' he said.

'It's a nice day,' she said.

'I said it was a nice day,' he said.

'I know. It's nice. I said it was nice,' she said.

J's coffee was cold when he got around to drinking it. Laura and he left the café before the sun went in, before Laura wanted to, and before the father finished playing with his girl.

2010: WHY ARE YOU HERE?

J saw that Laura's shoes were by the door. He called her name through the house and waited. She came through and said, 'Why are you here?'

'Good afternoon to you too. Sometimes I come home for lunch, you know that.'

'You didn't tell me. You've never told me that.'

'Why are you here?' he said.

'You never told me you come home for lunch.'

He removed his shoes and left them at the door, one of his on one of hers.

'How long have you been coming home for lunch?' she said, aligning the shoes so they were next to each other and making both pairs face into the house.

He shrugged his shoulders and took a bowl from the cupboard.

'Is this something you've been doing for a while?' she said.

He filled the bowl with cereal. He smelled the milk before pouring it over his cereal, and tapped the top of the sugar pot with his spoon before deciding to not add sugar.

'You don't have to tell me anything,' she said.

'Because you already know?'

'I don't know anything. You don't have to tell me because you're an adult. That's what you said the last time, wasn't it? That you were an adult. And look how that worked out.'

He said, 'I think you're trying to annoy me. I think that you think I'll start opening up to you if I start getting annoyed, but I won't.'

'Because . . .'

'Because there's nothing to open up to,' he said, stopping himself, not wanting to contribute too heavily if there was to be an argument. She didn't have to be right about everything, he thought, and he wasn't going to let her be right about this lunch break.

'You're having cereal and nothing else?'

'I'm trying to lose weight. It's all part of that fitness thing we talked about, remember? Healthy body, healthy mind. And what are you having for lunch, since you came home and all? You're not cooking?'

'You think cereal is healthy?'

'Why are you here?' he said.

'You keep asking me that. Is there something wrong?'

'Only making conversation.'

'I came for some work I left.'

'Oh, I see. You're here for some work. Where's the work then?'

'You don't believe me?' she said.

'I'm just interested, since you've never forgotten anything in your life.'

'I forget things; I've come home for things before. And, you know, on each of those times I came home for some work or something, you were never once here. But you always come home from work, for lunch, apparently.'

She left to get a handful of exam papers. She brought them into the dining room and laid them on the table. He leaned over to look at the date. Two weeks old, which was a date that could work in her favour. 'So you've got a poor memory then, have you?' he said.

'I forget things sometimes . . . oh right, I'm realising now what you're going on about. Why don't you ever just say it?'

'It? I don't know what you fucking mean.'

He started to eat. She watched him finish his lunch and thought of leaving.

He looked up at her when his bowl was empty. 'If this is keeping an eye on me then don't.'

'I don't know what you mean.'

'I wouldn't need to come here to do that. I wouldn't need to leave the office. You think I would, but I wouldn't. I really wouldn't. You're so sure this is about that, aren't you?'

'Maybe coming home for lunch isn't about that, but the way you're talking to me is. You never used to do this,' she said.

'You realise, don't you, that I believed your reason for being here?'

'The phrasing of that sentence suggests you don't believe it.'

'But I didn't go on about it,' he said.

He made her feel like a splinter, coarsely clinging to him. She couldn't recall another occasion being asked to leave a room, not that she remembered if he had said it in as many words, but she was sure he had said words to that effect.

'And what's worse: saying what's on your mind or keeping

it quiet? J, it's the keeping quiet that caused all of this in the first place. You know, I'm going to go. I actually have to go. I should have gone ten minutes ago. But do what you want. You know best. Bye.'

Her footsteps from the front door to the car were somehow almost as loud as the slam of the front door behind her. He had assumed he would feel relief on hearing the car leaving the drive, but he didn't. He asked himself what it was all about. He started to seriously consider what she had said, all of those accusations. He couldn't believe them. All he wanted was to spend half an hour in the house on his own. He didn't want to eat, to drink, or to think; he wanted only to sit. He told himself that this was the reason, unsure if it was. But the silence was spoiled now. It was full of their argument as though they were still arguing. He looked over to an object the other side of the room. He told himself once more about his reason for coming home this lunch break.

'It's not what you think,' he said.

When he left the house, he saw a white kitten rubbing the back of its neck against a brick. He stepped closer to the kitten but it ran away after a moment's eye contact.

'Don't do that,' he said, a little louder than he had intended. It meant nothing anyway; the kitten had already gone by the time he'd spoken.

2012: OTHER COUPLES AREN'T THIS LUCKY

It was nearly quarter past five when J decided he'd had enough. He packed away a few things, threw a banana peel and a chocolate wrapper into the bin, said goodbye to three people he had been ignoring all week, and left. The train station was a ten-minute walk; he could make it in six if he wanted to. And if there was no line at the ticket machine, he could make the 17:29. He wondered how another eight hours of nothing had passed as he sat on the slow train home.

'Got the late train then,' Laura said, walking upstairs without looking at him.

He made a pot of tea and switched on the television. He thought about taking her a tea, but she knew where it was if she wanted one. He felt hungry, so made a second pot of tea to keep him going. When he returned to the living room with the fresh tea, he turned the television off and toyed with the day's crossword in the newspaper. When it was time, he stood at the foot of the stairs and said, 'Honey, we'll need to leave quite soon.'

She walked downstairs, securing an earring in her left ear.

Her elbow came close to a framed painting on the wall. They had bought it from an arts café on the first floor of a converted lighthouse in Plymouth.

'Honey?' she said.

'Careful,' he said.

'Graze?' she said, after moving her elbow a fraction further from the wall.

'That's right.'

'Half eight?'

'Eight,' he said.

'Eight?'

'Yes, eight,' he said.

'How was I to know it'd be earlier?'

'Earlier than what?'

She looked annoyed, having been asked a question that didn't require an answer. But she answered anyway. 'Than usual. Earlier than usual.'

'We don't usually go at half eight.'

'Are you listening to me at all? Earlier than usual. We *usually* eat later than eight.'

'Are we leaving or not?' he said with his hands in his pockets.

She walked past him and left the house.

'Happy birthday,' he breathed, closing the front door.

The restaurant had a dark orange glow to it that Laura thought was strange the last time they came. Behind the welcoming desk was whisky, vodka, wine from, it felt, every country in the world; there was gin, sherry, brandy, tequila, and even sake. J gave the *maître de* his name, maintaining fierce eye contact. Laura watched the circling and bobbing fish behind the glass, occasionally becoming distracted from the fish to trace a bubble's journey from the small pucker mouths of the fish to the quiet end near the ceiling of the tank.

'Pop,' she said.

'Come on,' J said, tapping Laura lightly on her elbow.

The *maître de* sat them at a table with their menus and told them a waiter would be with them soon. She asked if they were ready to order drinks. They both ordered lemonade. The waiter came. Laura thought she recognised him before she realised he only happened to look a bit like a pupil's father from the school. She realised he didn't look that much like the father at all, but they had the same unfortunate disfigurement with the tops of their ears. Both ears folded flat inwardly on themselves, as though the restaurant had ordered him from a catalogue but hadn't taken the time to fully unpack him. They ordered a starter to share and two main courses. J told the waiter to bring all of the courses at once if it was convenient.

'They always put us in this bit,' Laura said.

'I told you last time; they probably only use the raised section when they're busy.'

'They're never busy. I don't see why we can't ask to sit up there.'

'Don't worry about it.'

'I'm not.'

The waiter came with all three dishes. They thanked him. He asked if they wanted any sauces or anything else, and turned to leave. Then, as if remembering, he turned back and told them to enjoy their meals. They thanked the waiter once more and he left.

'Other couples don't do this. Well, we know, don't we? They can't. In a way, we're lucky,' J said.

'Shut up, will you? What are you talking about?'

'What?' he said.

'Other couples aren't this lucky.'

After a silence, within which he drank over half of his lemonade in one sip and listened to another table's cutlery being moved around, he said, 'My parents did fuck all.'

'And mine did?'

'That's not the point,' he said.

'No, that's not the point. Thought you might say that.'

He was about to start his meal, but he stopped when she waved for the waiter. J watched the waiter walk over, and when the waiter arrived he watched Laura instead. She said, 'Glass of red wine, please. Any. House is fine. Thank you.'

'Anything else?' the waiter said, looking at Laura, and then J, and then Laura again.

'No thank you,' she said.

'Do you still want the lemonade?' the waiter said.

She pushed the lemonade towards J and said, 'He'll drink it.'

The waiter walked away.

'Are you kidding?' J said, leaning forward.

'Did you see him writing it down? One glass of red wine. How difficult is that to remember?' she said.

'Are you fucking kidding? I said are you kidding, Laura?'

'You can't so I can't. That's fair. That's really fair,' she said.

The waiter came with her red wine.

'I've changed my mind. Can you take it away? I'm sorry. I'm really sorry.'

The waiter left with the wine.

'It's not his fault, poor boy. We should leave him a decent tip,' she said, thinking again of his folded ears.

'Yes, *we* should. I suppose we're equally to blame there,' he said.

She said, 'Our food will get cold.'

They ate.

They'd both had enough. A new waiter collected their plates.

'Your parents ate meals out,' she said.

He was quiet for a moment, trying to remember when he mentioned his parents. He remembered that he did, and said, 'Their first meal in a restaurant was Mum's fortieth. They may have had five meals out in their lifetime. This is my thirty-ninth.'

'Your thirty-ninth meal in a restaurant?' she said, laughing.

'My thirty-ninth birthday and some people don't celebrate birthdays like these in restaurants like this.'

'Birthdays like these?'

'Ones that don't mean anything. You know what I'm saying. I know you do. Most people only celebrate the special ones, ones that matter.'

'That's exactly the problem; don't you see? Nothing is special for us. Nothing matters.'

'I disagree.'

'Your food gets stuck in the same tooth every time you eat. Did you know that?'

The waiter came over and asked if they wanted to see the dessert menu.

'Yes, please,' Laura said. She ordered a tiramisu. He ordered another lemonade and returned to locating the food in his teeth, without, he thought, her noticing.

'You don't want a coffee,' she said.

'Okay, I will then, might as well.'

'Espresso, sir?' the waiter said.

'Sure. Thanks. Thank you.'

The waiter went away. Laura wanted to apologise for the

tooth remark. Too much time had passed for it to sound sincere, she thought, and he had found and dislodged the morsel anyway.

'All right?' she said.

'Yes.'

The waiter returned with the espresso and the tiramisu. She took three large spoonfuls and pushed the plate to the centre of the table.

'Can I finish it?' J said.

'I've had enough. Of course you can.'

'No. *Can I?*'

'Oh,' she said, before trying another small spoonful. She concentrated and said, 'I think it's okay.'

'Sure?'

'Pretty sure. Anyway, what does it matter? It wouldn't be enough to notice even if there is any.'

He finished his espresso and then tried some of the tiramisu.

'I'm not sure,' he said, and he couldn't help but watch the plate until the waiter finally took it away.

As they walked from the restaurant, she held his hand. He was sure it wasn't her intention, that it was a result of a kind of routine mechanism that played out on a subconscious level. Still, he was glad to hold her hand, and he deliberately said nothing as they walked to the car from fear she might realise and take her hand back.

'We're lucky,' he said, as they sat in the car.

'We're lucky?'

'Yes. We are,' he said.

'Are we? I swear that sometimes I think my life is only this: shower, get dressed, drive to work, work, drive home, and if we're eating out have another shower, get dressed and leave, and if we're not eating out, get in my pyjamas, cook and eat. And then I try to sleep.'

'Right, and that's true for most, isn't it? How is that different from the majority of people?'

'I hope to God it isn't an accurate description of most people's life.'

'What do you mean? I don't know what you mean.'

'Meaning. There you go, that's the word: meaning. Everything's in place, like you said, just like it is for most people, but we're missing a why. Most people have a why. Where's mine?'

'You don't like your job.'

'I don't mind my job. Anyway, do you like yours? Who likes their job?' she said.

'I think most people worry about exactly what you're worrying about. Things are complicated now. It's different now than it was with our parents, and their parents. More complicated. Less simple. Layered.'

'I don't know what you're talking about. I don't think you know what you're talking about. And I don't think I even know what I'm talking about. I don't know what I mean,' she said, and turning to him, she said, in a more lively voice, 'And it's your birthday, I'm sorry. But haven't we changed? Don't you think we've lost something?'

'How can you lose something you've never had?' he said, choosing this moment to start the car's engine and pull away from their space.

'As if you just said that. Say it again.'

'How can you lose something you've never had?'

She was sure after hearing it the first time that he was talking about the child they never had, but after hearing it the second time, she didn't know what he meant. She had a strong feeling she would eventually ask him to explain himself. Whether this would happen during the drive home or later in bed or even the following week sometime, she didn't know, but despite feeling as though it was the last thing she wanted to talk about, she was going to ask him about it. She felt like she imagined one of her misbehaving children at school must feel like as they speak out of turn and argue with a teacher. They know they can't win against a teacher, not really, and they know it will only lead to more upset, but they insist on arguing anyway. It was the comparison with her misbehaving children that calmed her, but what he had said still nagged. What did he mean? She couldn't think of any way to bring it up without risking an argument, and, if there was to be one, the risk of being labelled as the lead protagonist and driving force behind the argument. J would have assumed she wanted to argue all along.

'I hate the way we argue. I don't know why we argue,' she said, after entering their bedroom, having brushed her teeth.

'Everyone argues,' he said.

'It should be so easy not to though. I hate myself when we argue. I know it sounds like it's you I hate when we're arguing, but it isn't; it's me I hate. So why can't I stop? You'd think I'd want to stop. You'd think some kind of natural reflex would keep me from acting in a way that makes me hate myself. Take evolution, for example. We know that hating oneself can lead to suicide, which means that surely any behaviour that leads to me disliking myself should be worked out. It isn't right. It's unnatural, surely.' She wished she hadn't used the word unnatural. She thought again about how unnatural she felt and had felt for a long time.

'It's true. Try not to worry though. There are things that I hate about myself when it comes to you, but it doesn't make any sense to dwell on these things,' he said.

'What things? And please don't make that face. It might help to tell me.'

'Okay. I hate—and this is the thing I really hate most of all—that I hear exactly what's wrong with you, and I know exactly why you're upset, why we're upset, but I give the impression that I don't know.'

'Why?'

'Why do I hate it or why do I do it to begin with?'

'Both,' she said.

'I hate it because it's like lying, because it *is* lying. I do it because it's the easiest way to avoid talking about what I don't want to talk about. I know it's difficult for you to say certain things straight up. I used to help and second-guess what I thought you meant. I'm not telling you anything you don't know, I suppose. I'd help and then we'd get to the bottom of whatever it was. But recently, your inability to say certain things about certain topics has turned into an excuse for me to deliberately misinterpret your best efforts to say anything.'

'Do you think we could both stop?'

'We can stop,' he said, because he agreed with everything she had said, but part of him knew that she'd only wake tomorrow and remember the conversation as another one of those dreamlike ones, so easy to have with the lights off. Lying in that bed, tired and in the dark, they'd planned so many holidays they never even came close to booking.

1995: WILL YOU PLEASE JUST TELL ME WHAT'S WRONG?

Laura noticed her dad first. 'Wondered where you got to,' she said.

'What's that, sweetheart?'

'Your train arrived five minutes ago.'

'Those steps,' he said.

'Hi Mum . . . look a bit pale. You okay?'

'Didn't like the journey.'

'You okay though?'

'Yeah, course I am. Still breathing, aren't I?'

'I wish you wouldn't say that.'

'You've no sense of humour. That's your problem.'

'Okay, thanks for that. Anyway, J's in the car. Shall I get him, Dad? For the bags?'

'It's okay. Not far, is it? The car?'

The ten-minute drive was quiet, except for the sound of Laura's mum catching her breath. Laura showed her parents around her new place.

'It's lovely.'

'Thanks, Dad. We've still got a few things to do.'

'No. Looks lovely.'

They went upstairs, taking their time. Laura knew it would've been her dad to say something nice. This upset her until she remembered her mum could do worse than not say anything.

'And this'll be your room. J, can you bring the bags?'

'Where's the bathroom?'

'Down the hall, Mum. The door's open.'

Laura left her mum and dad upstairs and sat with J. She leaned over him to put on some music. He rubbed her lower back. She played Louis Armstrong, music her dad liked. He came downstairs, smoking.

'Some Louis, eh?' he said. He sat on their new sofa.

J was looking at Laura, waiting for her to say something. Robert was dragging on his cigarette and the ash was about to fall. Robert turned his hand over and tipped the ash into his palm. Laura looked at her mum, hoping she would compliment the house. Laura noticed how tired her mum looked.

'Have you eaten?' Laura said.

'We had something,' she said.

'You look a bit tired.'

'Just the journey, be okay in a few minutes.'

'Okay, Mum. What would you like for dinner?'

Laura let the silence breathe for her parents to think.

'Don't mind, sweetheart. Fish and chips, to save you cooking?' Robert said.

'Yeah, I don't mind. J?'

'Yeah, that's fine. Let me know when you want it and I'll get it. Anyone like a drink? Robert, Catherine?'

'Tea would be lovely. Thanks dear.'

'I'll make a pot,' J said.

Laura said, 'I will. Has to be ridiculously strong.'

Robert stood and walked to other side of the room. He opened the window and threw out the ash and the butt.

J whispered to Laura, 'My herb garden's under that window.'

'Come on, Dad, let's go outside to smoke.'

'You're not smoking,' J said.

'Are you telling me I can't or asking if I am?' she said.

'You don't smoke,' he said.

'I'll just have one with my dad.'

They walked outside and shut the door so the smoke wouldn't travel into the house.

'Here you go,' he said.

'Thanks, but I've got my own.'

'Really?'

'I smoke sometimes.'

'But J doesn't know.'

'Only smoke alone, really, and it's honestly like almost never.'

'I only visit the bookies when I'm on my own and it's almost never as well. You and J have been together a while now.'

'Yeah.'

'Thought about marriage?'

Laura laughed. 'No. Why? I'm in my twenties, Dad.'

Robert waited for Laura to look at him.

'I'd love to see your mam see you married.'

'And what does that mean?'

'Only . . . that it's important to . . . and we might not . . . and it's just that I'd love to see your mam see you married.'

Laura understood. She put her hand over her mouth.

'Sweetheart, don't cry. Come here,' he said.

'Don't want to hear about it right now, please.'

Laura went inside, up to the bathroom. She came downstairs fifteen minutes later. 'J, why don't you show my dad your radios?' she said.

'Sure.'

They left the room. Laura sat next to her mum.

'You okay, dear?'

'Just tired, Mum.'

'Go to bed if you want.'

'Soon, but I want to talk to you.'

'About what?'

'I think you know.'

Catherine stopped in long concentration, looking as though she might be bringing to mind the faces of everyone she had ever met. Laura put her hand over her mouth. She looked away, waiting for her mum to speak. She thought they were going to sit there in silence for as long as it took J and her dad to return. Then her mum spoke.

'Darling, everyone . . . eventually has to . . . go.'

'That's not telling me anything.'

'You need to be patient. Don't get angry.'

'Will you please just tell me what's wrong?'

Catherine didn't answer.

Laura said, 'Perhaps you could say it in one word? If it's what I think it is then you could.'

'We all . . . expire . . . you know.'

'I know that. Christ! I'm making some tea.'

Laura stiffened herself for her mum's biting reply, but instead came a pathetic effort.

'Thanks, dear.'

The poor strength of her words said more than her heavy breathing and slow walking had done.

Robert came through first. 'Some lovely radios, sweetheart,' he said.

'What's that?' Catherine said.

'J collects radios, some lovely old ones. You should see.'

'Can show you if you like,' J said.

Laura came in with two teas. 'Bring one of the old ones in, J,' she said.

She poured her dad a tea and J came in with his Grunow tombstone radio. To Catherine, it looked more like an electric heater than a radio. It had an orange wooden glow. And although it resembled a tombstone, there was too much warmth about it for the association with death to be fitting. J turned it on to find The Beatles, *Love Me Do.*

J looked up at Robert and Catherine. 'This okay?' he said.

They nodded. Robert tapped his left knee as he held his tea in his right hand. He spilt some tea on his trousers, but no one noticed. Catherine never liked The Beatles, but something about the crackled veil of the radio's performance made it sound familiar. She sat still as she listened, but she was enjoying herself as much as anyone else around the radio. The reception fell away into a sea of crackles and static. J leaned forward to fiddle for reception, but it worked itself out. It was the opening of *Wouldn't It Be Nice* by The Beach Boys. Catherine lent back into the sofa and said, 'Oh, I did like The Monkees.'

Laura controlled a laugh into a smile. The radio played as they ate their fish and chips and until they said goodnight.

Laura and J were in the dining room, sharing a pot of tea. Last week, she had told J she wanted her mum to see how the sun burst into the living room in the morning. It was something mum would have liked, she had thought.

'Do you think we should wake them?'

'Better let them sleep, I suppose. Mum's tired.'

'Is she okay?'

'Yeah.'

'I'm hungry,' J said.

'Toast okay?'

'Sure.'

Robert came downstairs at ten past ten and wished Laura and J a good morning.

'Your mam'll be down in a bit,' he said.

'Bacon sandwich?'

'Lovely. Thanks, sweetheart.'

Laura put the bacon under the grill. Catherine came downstairs and apologised for sleeping so long. She said she didn't sleep well. Laura kissed her cheek.

'Lovely room though,' Robert said.

'Yes, lovely, just different,' Catherine said.

J came in with tea for four. He asked everyone what they'd like to do. He made some suggestions: the castle, the market, a walk.

'Not up to the walking, dear.'

'I could drive us for lunch somewhere,' J said.

'We understand you're not up to the walking, Mum. That's fine. But why exactly?'

'I can drive,' J said.

'J, can you check the grill for me?'

Robert walked over to the mute radio, still in the living room from last night. J came in with bacon sandwiches. He put a plate in front of Catherine and one in front of Robert.

'Thanks,' Robert said.

Catherine said, 'Thank you, but I'm afraid I don't think I'm up to eating anything right now.'

'That's okay,' J said.

Laura and Catherine sat there as quiet as the radio. Robert and J talked about football. Robert started smoking.

'Hold on, Robert.'

Robert looked up, unmoving and waiting.

J came in with an eggcup and said, 'Use this for an ashtray.'

'Thanks.'

After Robert finished his last mouthful, Laura saw her mum nudge him with her leg.

Laura laughed without smiling. 'Very subtle. Was that permission? Are you going to tell me now, Dad? I think you're allowed to. You got the nudge.'

Robert's face turned rigid. He hadn't looked at her this way since she was a child, acting up. It still worked to make her stop.

'We'll be off tomorrow, sweetheart.'

'You don't have to.'

'We know.'

'Why then?'

'Your mam needs her own bed.'

'Right . . . and why?' Laura walked out of the room, repeating the word *why*.

Catherine looked at J until she got his attention. 'You understand it's nothing about you. I don't want you to feel anything's wrong. I meant to say before, by the way, we're so glad about you two, together, and about the house and the way things seem to be going. It's a comfort. It's very nice, the house. We're proud. And, it goes without saying, we like you.'

Robert nodded.

'Thank you,' J said.

Laura came back. She had changed out of her pajamas and into some jeans and an old hooded jumper. Catherine turned to her and said, 'Let me explain.'

Laura didn't want to know. Was it tiredness? Or did she really not want to know? There was a pause and she thought one of her parents might speak. But they were waiting for Laura. She had to invite the news. A nod would do. But she couldn't. She then heard herself speaking. 'We can talk later.'

The four of them looked at the radio on the centre of the table.

'Lovely radio,' Robert said.

1991: ENDING

'Sorry, Laura. I slept completely wrong. Have you ordered? I'm sorry I'm late. I dreamt I was working on a farm—I'm not sure what kind of farm it was—and I woke with a pain in my foot. I was still wearing socks and when I rubbed the sole of my foot, you know, where the pain was, I felt something hard. When I touched my foot, it felt as though every bone in my entire body was broken. The pain shot up right through me. I took my socks off and it took me a long time because of the pain. Eventually, I removed them and the hard thing fell to the floor. It was a cherry. It had infected my foot and, to cut a long story short, I went to hospital and they removed my foot.'

'It sounds . . .'

'It was. It was horrible. That's what you were going to say, right? You know, I woke sweating. I never wake up sweating. What a horrible dream. Really.'

'You're still calling it a dream and not a nightmare though,' she said.

'Children have nightmares.'

'I have nightmares, sometimes.'

'You never tell me about them,' he said.

'Look, I'm really hungry. Shall we order or not?'

'Sorry, yeah, let's order.'

Their regular visits to *Tim's Café* began last year, on the day he promised to cook for Laura the first time. She had early lectures and was due to be home by eleven. He promised to have lunch ready for her return. He woke around quarter past ten with the intention of cooking, but when she returned twenty minutes later—earlier than expected—he suggested they go out for lunch, on him, and she agreed. He told her he was about to cook, but she was early. They walked until they came across the first place to eat. They both ordered a full English breakfast and she said it was the best she'd ever tasted. After that, they started to go to *Tim's* most Saturdays. They ordered their breakfasts and sat looking at each other. His dream was still on his mind. The waitress brought over one small pot of tea and one cup of coffee.

'You didn't want a tea?' he said.

'Coffee today. Didn't you hear me order?' she said.

'Guess not. Why coffee anyway? You tired?'

'A little.'

He poured himself a tea.

She said, 'You wouldn't believe how much I hate you interrupting me.'

'When did I?'

'Earlier, but it doesn't matter.'

The food came. It only ever took a few minutes, which was one of the reasons they liked this place. They talked about what they wanted to do that evening. They knew people who were going to *Twisters* later, and they were both open to going. It was a *Toss the Boss* night, so a chance the round would be half price. After ordering, the barman (rarely the boss) would toss a coin. If a customer called it correctly, their round of drinks would be half price. Laura often made J order their drinks on a *Toss the Boss* night. She either said that he was lucky or that she was unlucky; it depended on her mood.

'Shall we get a bottle to share before? To have with dinner,' he said.

'Okay, if it's white.'

'I was thinking red.'

'Rose then.'

'Really?'

'Only fair to meet halfway,' she said.

'I'd prefer white to rose.'

'So we'll get white then?'

'If you want,' he said.

'Well, I'm asking you. Shall we get white?'

'I wanted red, but white is okay,' he said.

'So white then?'

'Okay, white.'

They finished their breakfasts.

'Do you remember the time we ordered two?' she said.

'You're still hungry, aren't you?'

'I really am. I don't know what's wrong with me. Will you order another as well?'

'I don't think I'd manage it.'

'I can't sit here and eat alone.'

He said, 'I really can't. Don't be mad at me because I can't eat another breakfast.'

'I'm not,' she said.

'Let's order one more then, and we'll share it.'

He ate more than he wanted, trying to eat his half, but she still ate most of the breakfast.

'You make me look fat, not eating your half,' she said.

'I'm fed up of this. Do you realise what I did for you?' he said, wishing he hadn't.

'What?' she said. 'What did you do?'

'Don't worry about it.'

They walked back to his place. But as they arrived at his front door, she said, 'Think I'm going to go back to mine. Need to do some revision.'

'If you want,' he said. As she turned away, he said, 'But your books are at mine.'

'I'll get them later,' she said, before kissing him on the cheek and waving in the same short movement.

She walked to hers. He watched her first few steps before opening his front door. He called through the house, but there was no response. His housemate must have been at work. He called for his housemate again, only to listen. He sat at the living room table, a small table for two, flicking through a short story collection by Robert Walser. There was a story contained in one page so he read it. Only after he read it did he read the title: *The Boat*. One line of the story stuck with him: *No noise, no sound.*

He asked himself, *why write noise and sound? What's the difference between noises and sounds? Intention? Pleasantness? Clarity?* The superfluous and confusing detail of describing nothing twice caused him to smile. After a moment's thinking, it made complete sense to him. *No noise, no sound.* He put the book down and went into the kitchen to make tea. When he sat again at the small table, he thought of reading. He thought of listening to music. He drank the tea and focused on the quiet, trying to feel what Walser felt when he wrote those four words. He wanted Laura to be with him. He walked to hers.

The front door of her flat was unlocked. He let himself in and heard talking in the kitchen. He closed the door behind him and the talking stopped. He realised he would have to at least say hello now. He walked into the kitchen. Laura was there.

'Oh, hello,' he said.

She said goodbye to her flat-mates and asked J if he wanted to walk somewhere. He said he didn't mind. They walked towards the park.

'If you don't tell me, I won't speak to you,' she said.

He tried to find a line with conviction. Composing nothing, he told her the truth. 'I was seeing someone else. Until last week.'

'I'm going back.'

'Okay, but I'm coming too. I want to explain.'

'You've told me.'

'Yes, but I haven't explained everything. I'm coming with you.'

She turned and started walking back. He followed a step behind. He heard her sniff and wondered if she was crying, or trying not to. She sat on her bed and he by her desk.

'Explain then, if you really have to.'

'I was with her before I was with you.'

'And what's that mean? Why does that even matter?'

'Because, if anything, I was cheating on her with you and not on you with her. I know that sounds bad.'

'You sound bad.'

'And I'm not trying to sound good; I'm trying to be honest.

I *am* being honest. And I'm being honest because I care about you.'

'You're choosing me? Is that what you're telling me?'

'I've chosen you.'

'And I should feel lucky?'

'There's no *should* except that I'm telling you this because I absolutely *should*. I *should* have told you earlier. There's no specific way I expect you to feel. I had no intention before I started speaking except that I *should* tell you.'

'Well now you've done what you *should*. You've told me.'

'She lives in another city, by the way. Do you want me to leave now?'

'I don't know.'

'Okay, I don't know either,' he said. 'Actually, I am going to go. You need to think. That's obvious.'

She stood and rested into his body. He put his arms around her. She stretched and kissed him. He pulled away and said, 'I can come over later, or you can come to mine, and we can talk. Will I see you tonight?'

She nodded.

'So, either way, I'll see you tonight?' he said.

'Either way,' she said, deepening her voice to imitate J.

'You know what I mean?'

'But I still don't like to hear you say it. You could sound a little more bothered.'

'Trust me, I am bothered. I only told you in the first place because I'm bothered. You wouldn't have ever known.'

Those last five words made her realise she needed to think about it, and he needed to go.

'Okay,' she said, and he left.

She cried when the front door closed. She thought of going

into the kitchen again, but no matter how lonely she felt, she didn't want to be with anyone. She realised this earlier, as she sat with her flat-mates. It was almost a relief when J came over, taking her away from a larger company and into his, as much as it was a relief when he left, leaving her alone. She hated him for this. She realised she needed to know more, however upsetting it might be. But going to him then would have been too early, so she waited.

He had a book in his hand as he answered the door.

'Were you reading?'

'No. Well, yes, I was, but not really. Come in.'

She remained still, as though he hadn't invited her inside. 'I'm here because there's something I should have asked,' she said.

He let his silence play as encouragement as he waited.

'I want you to tell me why you liked me, why you wanted me in the first place, since you already had someone.'

'It's difficult,' he said.

'No it isn't,' she said, and the words came like rain. 'It's easy if it's real. I know why I liked you. I liked you, to begin with, because of the way you sat in that wooden chair in the concourse, how it made you look too tall for any room. It didn't matter how tall the ceiling was, you still looked too tall. Your shoulders angled towards your feet, your palms facing in. So there, it's easy. If you don't know then how do I know it's real, that you're real. And your answer should be better than mine. I was single. You obviously weren't.'

'I noticed the past tense: why you *liked* me, not *like* me.'

'Tell me what I want to know, please.'

'Come in,' he said.

'Not until you tell me.'

'Aren't you cold?'

She waited.

He couldn't say it was because she looked a little bit like Jodie Foster. Besides, he'd already told her a few months ago and she couldn't see the similarity. He felt unworthy and realised it was the first time he had ever felt this way in her presence. Then he knew what to say. 'Because I feel good with you. You always make me feel important and wanted. I just feel good. It's simple, but that's it.'

They went inside.

'I hated the quiet before you came,' he said. 'No noise, no sound.'

She didn't say anything, not wanting to admit she felt the same.

'How do people sit quietly?' he said.

'I still have some questions.' The questions came to her fluently and she asked them without thinking them through. She made him answer everything. She even asked about Rebecca's parents. J admitted he liked her parents and he would miss them more than he would miss Rebecca. This upset Laura most of all.

She realised she had asked everything she needed. Somehow—she didn't know why—she felt better. She played with two potential reactions: He was either easier to trust because people who had made mistakes are easier to trust than people who hadn't, or he was not to be trusted because some people never change. She tried to ignore it.

'You can't do anything like this again.'

'I won't,' he said, before she finished speaking.

'All right, I feel silly now, all this talking.'

'I'll put something on.'

He played a Prince record and they sat and listened. The background of music and not quiescence gave her the new confidence to say what was on her mind without embarrassment. 'You think we'll grow old together?' she said.

'I hope so.'

'We won't if you keep playing Prince.'

'What do you want on instead then?'

She said, 'Bowie, *Low*.'

He played it and returned to her.

She said, 'You said you hope so when I asked if we'll grow old together. But what do you really think? What you want and what you think are different.'

'I hope and I think we will. It's what all this has been about. I feel different now, the world feels changed.'

They listened to three songs before she said, 'You said the world is different.'

'I said it seems changed, it feels different.'

'Okay. But am I different? Sorry, do I *seem* or *feel* different or changed to you?'

'You're the same. I feel right with you. But I think you know that. I've already told you.'

'Do you blame me for wanting to hear it again?' she said.

'Not one bit. I agree, it sounds good. It's okay to repeat the good things, like what you said earlier: we're going to end up together, we're going to end up together.'

End, ending. She gave the words space, but they still didn't fit. Her expression was *growing old*; she never said anything about ending up together. But she was a little tired, and anyway, his intentions were the same. The album finished, so she hurried her thoughts to a close too. Ending or growing: they were the same, weren't they?

2015: WELL, IS IT FINISHED?

'That was nice, wasn't it, watching those films? It was like remembering, in a way,' she said.

'You slept through most of them.'

'I think I dreamt of the places we lived, parks we walked through, things like that. I slept, but it was still nice,' Laura said, switching the kettle on.

A breeze sent a whistle through the house and almost gave her a headache. She knew exactly where it came from. It took her mind to the time she tried to leave the boyfriend she had before J, so many years ago. This was the only relationship she had ever broken. She remembered having no idea how to do it. She had said everything she thought she needed to say, and she started to walk out. She could tell from her first tentative step that she was going to turn around.

'So?' she remembered saying.

There was a whistling noise, and the house was the only one with something to say. She sat, but left her coat on. It was only half a gesture, like choosing to kiss someone for the first time but only with closed lips. He didn't know how long she was staying. She could tell by the way he was biting his fingernails. She didn't know if she wanted to kiss him. She only knew she wanted to not want to. 'I really love this house,' she said.

He started to say something, but she cut him off. 'No. Don't,' was what she said. And he yielded. Of course he did. So they sat there, and listened to the house's whistling.

She had more to say, but each new silent second was a display of her control. She waited another minute, maybe another two. When her heart started to take her to those evenings in bed when she couldn't sleep, with only his breathing and the house's whistling for company, she decided it was time to speak again.

'I didn't like it to begin with. The first time I came here—do you remember that first time?—I thought it looked like a sad house. I told you at the time, do you remember? You never cleaned. It was dark. Then I noticed these little things. I found our bakery, with our bread and our doughnuts. I couldn't believe it was only two minutes away. I felt lucky. You stopped thanking me for buying them, did you realise that? But I don't want to talk about that. I loved this house. Do you hear? That whistling noise solved my sleeping problems. The best thing though was the sun setting right in the middle of our window. It felt like a torch pointing right at our house, right into our room, at us.'

She realised she should have left earlier. The best time would have been when she had started to leave.

'Can I speak now?' he said.

She composed herself by straightening her back against the chair on which she read poetry and drank coffee on Sunday mornings, when he was still in bed. 'You said the last meaningful thing you will ever say to me last night,' she said.

'So that's it?'

'I think so,' she said, looking around. 'I really loved this place.'

'You realise this is my place, don't you? It's in my name. I was here long before you came here, and I'll be here for a good while yet. I'm not exactly okay with you hanging around just so you can see the house for a bit longer.'

'You're a fucking jerk, do you know that?'

She left the house after that, and never physically visited it again. She often wondered if she would have broken up with him had he not been so aggressive about her loving the house more than she loved him. Laura left these thoughts and poured the tea.

'Thanks,' J said.

'You know, we haven't spoken to Si for a long time. We should ask him over or something.'

'Interesting idea.'

'J.'

'Yes.'

'He wasn't . . . I don't know . . . *right.* It's not like you don't know why. It's not like he did anything wrong. None of us were right. I used to cook meals for him and little Jessie. She'd go off and watch a film and Simon and I would talk. All night. Perhaps you believed I was playing with Jessie. I wasn't. I was with him. We could be in contact still.'

J kept his thoughts to himself. As far as he was aware, the period during which none of them were right had left nothing to glean. A conversation entered his mind. He remembered sitting with Simon in his house, drinking a coffee after an evening out. There was a silence, as there often was with Simon, so J felt responsible to make conversation.

'I don't know what I'm doing sometimes,' J said, wanting to say more but losing focus.

Simon was looking at his feet, as usual. 'Okay,' Simon said.

J tried to be more specific and said, 'I'm not making much money. My friends have better jobs. I don't know.'

'Your friends?' Simon said.

'Sometimes I worry about the future, about . . .'

'Okay, stop. Listen,' Simon said, almost laughing.

J did listen, but that was a different Simon.

'J.'

'Yes,' he said, looking up at Laura.

'I really believed you were leaving me. I don't know what I'd have done.'

'Well I'm not, and I never thought about it.'

'You've thought about it, you must have,' she said.

'Why say something like that?'

'I'm not trying to argue. We're adults. We can talk about it. But you've thought about leaving me, haven't you? Even if it was a long time ago, you've thought about it at least once. You must have.'

He wasn't prepared to speak about it. He felt that she must have considered leaving him, and he wondered when. But it still wasn't worth getting into. These things never are.

'I'm sorry, but I really don't think this is a good idea,' he said.

'So you have thought about it?'

'Because I didn't say no?'

'Yes, and it's okay. Really, it is.'

J didn't answer, deciding to decide this time. He walked to the window and swore at the rain. The patterns it made on the glass were the only thing J liked about rain. As a child, he used to watch the windows of the car or train when it was raining. Some beads of rain would join other beads and run the entire length of the window together, gladly random and unhurried, but some would bounce off into the road or onto the train track, alone. Each bead was different. He didn't know what to say to Laura. He understood her frustration. She was half bored and half frightened, but what could he do about it? He started to walk towards her, not knowing what he was going to do or say, but thinking that simply walking towards her was the important movement. They would then take a path together like two rain drops, without thinking and with an unexplained momentum behind them. Or he would bounce off and fall onto the tracks. He cleared the tracks from his mind and thought about one foot in front of the other, because, he reminded himself, that was the important thing.

'I'm going to call him. He should be our oldest friend,' she said, picking up the phone. She dialled his house number, hoping he hadn't moved.

'Who, Simon? What will you say?'

'I'll see if he wants to have dinner with us one evening or something.'

The phone was ringing.

J said, 'How *should* a person be an old friend? Surely they are or aren't. There's no *should*.'

Laura would have replied if not for the dial tone.

'Hello,' Simon said, his voice sounding as though it had travelled through the bark of a tree to reach her.

'Simon? It's me, Laura. How are you?'

'Fine. And you?'

'Okay. It's been a long time.'

'It has,' he said.

'J and I were thinking it'd be nice to do something.'

'Like what?'

'We could go out for a meal on the weekend.'

'I'm not sure.'

'You could pop over for tea.'

'Perhaps.'

'What would you like to do, Simon?'

'I'm not sure. It's been years.'

'Why don't you have a think and call me back? We're free this weekend, so whatever you want to do is fine.'

'Okay, well, there's no need to call back. We can arrange it now, I suppose. Why not? How about here, at mine, this weekend? Saturday.'

'Sure. What time?'

'Sometime in the afternoon. Anytime that's good for you. I'm free.'

'Okay, that's great, Simon. We're looking forward to it already.'

'See you then,' he said.

'We'll call you later in the week to confirm.'

'Why?'

'I'm not sure,' she said.

'Come over Saturday if you're coming. There's no need to phone.'

'You're right. I'm not sure why I said that.'

'Saturday then?' he said.

'See you then.'

Simon hung up the phone.

'Bloody hell,' Laura said. She put the kettle on and topped up the teapot.

'Okay?' J said.

'Yes. We're going over Saturday afternoon,' she said, before repeating the other details of the conversation: what he said, what she said. She was like this with books. She felt greatly for the characters and, after reading the book, wanted to tell someone about them more than anything. She would approach a friend and tell them how great the book was and how much she hated or loved the main character. The friend would ask Laura why she hated or loved them, but all she could do was repeat the plot. She heard herself doing this, but that didn't make a difference. There was no way to express how she felt. Although this frustrated her, she saw the exclusivity of her feelings for a character as a significant part of what made her feelings great.She poured the tea.

Laura thought about the tone of Simon's voice. She was set to tell J about it until she realised how small a difference it was. She wondered if it was age and nothing else.

'Probably,' she said, listening to her own voice.

'What?'

'Nothing.'

'I suppose it would be interesting to see him again,' J said.

This was as much as she could hope for. She said, after a moment, 'There are too many people we've lost contact with.'

'It's normal. We can't see everyone we used to know.'

'We don't see anyone we used to know.'

'It's normal.'

'Not in this case. After what happened, we should have made sure.'

'Of what?' he said.

'That he was okay.'

'What happened was why we couldn't see him. We tried, for over a year.'

'We didn't try hard enough,' she said.

'How long should we have tried to stay in his life while at the same time knowing he didn't want us to?'

'Trying harder doesn't mean trying for a longer amount of time.'

'The way I see it, it's simple: he didn't want to see us,' he said.

'He didn't want to see us the way we were. We could have been other people.'

'I'm not sure you even know what you mean by that. He didn't want to see us or anyone.'

'You don't know that.'

'Okay, maybe he wanted to want to see us. But he stopped wanting to see anyone, except, I hope, Jessie, of course. We tried, but it didn't work.'

'We tried, but it didn't work,' she repeated, because the sentence sounded too large for her not to say. 'They could write that on my gravestone,' she said.

He raised his eyebrows.

She said, 'I know it didn't work, but we can try again now, can't we?'

The short time it took to drive to Simon's made them feel ashamed. Laura blamed herself for losing his friendship. J thought about the birthdays and Christmases and wished he had at least dropped a card through the letter box. He thought about the anniversary of the accident and felt he should have come with flowers. He wouldn't have had to say anything, and there would have been no need for a note, even. He could have gone over after work and asked Simon how he was, handed him the flowers, and left.

Simon answered the door smiling. 'Come in. I imagine it's much the same as the last time you were here.'

'This is different,' Laura said, pointing to a dressing table.

'It wasn't there before?' Simon said, looking to J with a seriousness that felt forced.

'I'm not sure. The garden looks nice.'

Simon made a pot of tea to drink in the back garden. Simon talked about Sarah with a new freedom. He spoke about the time they met, the meals they used to cook for each other, and even about the first time she stayed with him overnight. At the back of Laura's mind though, there was something still not right with him, but, she thought, having experienced what he experienced, expecting him to be one day better and as he used to be was expecting too much. At least they were all speaking about her, which couldn't have happened before.

'Do you and Jess talk much about Sarah?' Laura said.

'Sometimes, we do. Anyway, how about you two?'

'What? When we first spent the night together?' J said.

'No, of course not,' Simon said, and J wondered why Simon couldn't tell it was a joke. 'Your first shared meal, or something like that.'

Laura said, 'It was a disaster. I made shepherd's pie, but the meat was overdone because I was so worried about poisoning him, and the potato was too buttery. It was really terrible, but he still ate it anyway.'

'Did you?' Simon said.

J nodded, and said to Laura, 'That wasn't the first meal you cooked me though.'

'It was.'

'It wasn't. It was pizza, or what you thought was pizza. Do you remember? You topped slices of bread with tomatoes and cheese and put them in the oven. It was more like soggy cheese on toast. At Rowan Close, remember?'

'The shepherd's pie was first. That's what we always say.'

'It wasn't. It doesn't matter.'

Laura looked at the floor in thought. She said, 'It was the pizza, wasn't it? Why have you let me say it was the shepherd's pie all this time, for years? We always tell people that, and you've never said anything before.'

'It doesn't matter,' J said, and Simon agreed that it didn't.

It was hearing Simon that convinced Laura to give this one up. She went to the bathroom and made a joke of asking if it was still in the same place.

J asked if there was any more tea, and Simon went to make a fresh pot.

Laura returned. 'Where's Simon?'

'Making tea. Didn't you pass him?'

Simon came through with the fresh tea and poured. Laura, feeling it was her responsibility to fill the silence, forgot about first meals. She started a conversation about the local football team. It was one of those nervous reactions she couldn't understand. After a while, Simon said, as though they were on the subject, 'I think a lot of how we would have been now, Sarah and I.'

'And what do you think about?' J said.

'I don't know. It's difficult. Impossible, even. You hear these stories of couples. They go wrong, don't they? Everything is fine for years, and then wham.'

Neither J nor Laura had anything to say, so Simon continued. 'I knew this one couple. Terrible story. Really quite sad.'

'What happened?' Laura said.

'It's a long story.'

J said, 'We've got time.'

'It's not that long, actually. But it's not such a positive story.'

'You already said it was terrible,' Laura said. 'Tell us.'

'As you wish. The night we first met them, the couple in question, Sarah and I had fallen out over something. Only something little, nothing at all. We had both known David for a while, and we knew he'd found a serious girlfriend at last. This would be the first time we would meet them together. Both of us expected nothing from them. David had had girlfriends before, and I wondered if he might have had another girlfriend then as well, you know, at the same time. Some people do that, don't they? Anyway, David's relationships were short, but he was only, I can't remember how old exactly, but in his early twenties or a number close to that. Thinking about it, he must have been almost thirty. I can't remember anything anymore. Anyway, Sarah and I were different to him in most respects. We were serious from the start. I felt we were like two birds, meeting mid flight or something.'

'I thought something similar with me and J except that we met mid fight.'

J and Simon laughed, and then it was quiet.

Simon said, 'I always felt we were special, Sarah and I.'

'You were,' J said.

'What about this David then?' Laura said.

'Well, he was someone we knew pretty well, but when he introduced us to this girl, Kate, he changed in a second. They looked right together, and he looked different. I'm not sure if he acted differently but, at the time, I believed he did. It was one of those funny things. Part of me resented him for changing, because Sarah and I never had to change to be with each other.'

Laura said, 'Changing a bit is okay, sometimes. It can be healthy.'

'That's what I was about to say. Part of me resented him, but mostly, a much bigger part of me, thought it was probably a good thing. Some people need to change to fit with each other, and some people naturally fit. If he had to change a little then this was probably a good thing. But I'm not sure about his change. Maybe he didn't change. Maybe it was just another side to him, one I hadn't seen.'

'It was probably that,' J said.

'I think so. He was acting more comfortable in himself. I felt more comfortable with Sarah when we were alone, but he seemed comfortable all of the time. Well, I presume he felt comfortable with Kate when they were alone. They were living together within two months and married in six.'

'Doesn't sound like a sad—or what was it you said—*terrible* story, Simon,' Laura said.

Simon carried on as if Laura hadn't interrupted. 'We saw them every now and then and, after five years, he told us they were divorcing.'

'Why?' Laura said, leaning forward.

'She was divorcing him. Apparently, she'd had an affair, and when it was over, David told Kate that he knew and he had forgiven her. He knew the whole time, and he told her this. When she asked him how he knew, he told her the reasons. I don't need to go into this with you though. Things were awkward between them but, as far as he was aware, things were no different than they had been, since he knew she was being unfaithful. He could see that Kate had changed, but he put it down to guilt, which, I suppose, was completely natural. Both natural of him to think, and also it would have been a natural reaction, wouldn't it? Guilt.'

J wondered why Simon was telling them this. He couldn't remember how it came up in conversation. Didn't he start talking about it for no reason?

Simon continued. 'David told both Sarah and I that they were in bed together that night and they didn't speak. She woke him up at three o'clock. He said he couldn't remember if he was asleep or not, but he remembered opening his eyes to her hand on his shoulder. He didn't feel nervous or uneasy. He thought she might apologise. He thought they might clear the air and make up. He was almost excited, he said. But she said she was leaving him. They spoke for hours. He said it was the most tiring night of his life. She said a lot, but the main reason behind her deciding to leave was that if he didn't love her enough to leave her for her cheating on him then she shouldn't be with him. Imagine that. Because he didn't leave her, she left him. He wondered if he should have done something to put an end to their affair, but she didn't leave David because he didn't try to stop her cheating. She said this. She said she still wouldn't have felt that he cared enough. I was amazed. You know, we hardly see him anymore. I mean, *I* hardly see him. I'm not sure what would have happened if that same thing had happened to Sarah and I. Well, it wouldn't have happened anyway, would it?'

J wanted to leave. Laura broke the silence. 'You and Sarah weren't perfect, Simon.'

'Didn't say we were.'

'It's how you go on about the two of you the whole time.'

'When did I say we were perfect? To whom have I said that?'

'Like the whole bird comment, and then talking about other couples who weren't like you. The birds thing was correct by the sound of it, the two of you meeting in the air, and what was it you said, meeting mid flight, yes, that's probably right, looking down on everyone else.'

'That's unfair. When the hell did I say we were perfect?'

'I think we should leave,' Laura said. J stood, nodded to Simon because he didn't know what to do, and followed Laura out of the house, into the car.

'Why didn't you ever say about the shepherd's pie?' she said, in the driveway of their house, having been silent during the short drive.

'What do you mean?' J said.

'You know what I mean. Why now?'

'Let's just get inside.'

'Don't tell me then, but I really don't understand why,' she said.

She let herself in and walked upstairs. He soon followed and sat at the kitchen table. Everything was still until she came down again, a few minutes later. She sat at the table. The palm of her left hand was flat against its surface. She lifted each finger in turn to point up as far as it could, comparing each finger's flexibility until they stopped looking like fingers but parts of a machine.

The light rain could be heard on the car's roof in the driveway if he concentrated hard enough. J was sure he could see the sun slowly moving as it set. After the third time Laura mentioned the shepherd's pie, J decided to return to Simon's alone. It was getting dark, but it had to be that day.

He said, 'Feel like cooking, let's cook tonight.'

'That a joke?'

'No, really. I really feel like some shepherd's pie, don't you?'

She walked upstairs and he left the house. The air outside was soft and the rain was more like condensation from a cup of tea than real rain. He remembered the time he came home, close to when they first moved in together, and the front door was off its hinges. She was standing in the hallway. He looked at the door, at her, and the door again. She was crying and before he said anything, she said, 'I opened it, nothing more.'

He lined the door against the frame and swore. He couldn't remember what he said exactly, but remembered saying it quietly.

She said, again, 'I opened it.'

They talked about money, and she wouldn't stop apologising.

Simon answered the door. 'Yes,' he said.

J walked inside, sat in the living room and waited.

'Remember that time I lent you that lawnmower, years and years ago, when you borrowed that lawnmower of mine.'

'Yes,' he said.

'Nice of me to lend that to you, wasn't it?'

Simon went to the kitchen and put the kettle on. J waited. Simon returned and said, 'What is it you want?'

'A chat.'

'Not much of a chatty person, nor am I much in the mood for a chat.'

'You borrowed that CD of mine once, didn't you? That Elvis' greatest hits CD. We were playing it at the house one day. That was the first CD Laura and I ever bought. Nice of us to lend that to you, wasn't it?'

Simon couldn't make eye contact, but found enough of something to be able to speak. 'I know you know, all right.'

'You don't know as much as you think you do.'

'Tell me what you want to tell me and then leave. I'm in no mood for riddles.'

J stood and said, 'Work it out.'

There was some quiet and J wondered if he would leave.

But Simon said, 'I recognised someone the other day, an old friend. Nicole. I saw her in the town and stopped her by tapping the back of her elbow. She turned quickly, and from how I remembered her it was strange for her to be so tense. But it was Sarah who knew her better than I, so what do I know?'

'You talk a lot more than you used to,' J said.

Simon sat, and continued to talk, 'We started to talk, Nicole and I, about the small things, like work and weather, and even football. I didn't think Nicole knew anything about football, but perhaps one of her boys had gotten into it. They would be the right age for it now. As I started to relax into the conversation, I started to remember the long evenings that Nicole and her husband, Terry, and Sarah and I spent together. There was something like intimacy on those evenings, and I felt it returning to me, right there. So I told Nicole that it was Sarah's birthday.'

J said, 'When was that?'

'Last Wednesday. Anyway, I told her this and all she did was put her hand near her mouth. Laura does something similar, doesn't she, with her hand, but hers is far more elegant, childlike. Nicole looked to be receiving an electric shock. Then I made a joke, in an attempt to make things light again, about the weather. Not a funny joke but a joke nonetheless. I told her how typical the sun was, and that it always rained on my birthday but never on Sarah's. I soon realised that I shouldn't have said anything. I tried to change the subject, to anything but Sarah, but Nicole spoke over me. She said: *yes, yes, I know, yes, yes.* I stopped talking, seeing as though Nicole wasn't listening to me. Then she said that everything was confusing at the moment. I asked her what she meant, and I told her I wasn't confused. I thought about the way she was stopping me speaking and it was obvious that she wanted to stop me mentioning Sarah. I noticed she didn't mention Sarah's name when she could have done. I told her I had to be somewhere, and I went.'

'Some people can't talk,' J said.

'You're telling me. When she left, I went into a type of anger. I felt like saying to her: *you can say her name. You know her name. I know her name. You can say her name. You can say "Sarah" in my presence and I won't break down in tears. I am someone to whom you can say "Sarah". You can say "Sarah" and nothing bad will happen. It won't cause you any embarrassment to say "Sarah". It won't cause me any more pain to hear someone else say "Sarah". I say it aloud to myself at least two times a day. I can't count the number of times I think her name in my head. When I think about her and when I speak her name, I don't picture her in the road and I don't picture her in pain. When I think about her and when I speak her name, I picture everything but her death, her murder. I think of when we made love, when we shared meals, when we sat with Jessica, and I think about all those wasted hours spent sleeping. That's what I think about the most. I wish I hadn't slept so many hours. People say they regret the crossed words and the fights, but I don't. They're too inevitable to be regrettable. But I could have stayed up an extra hour a night, or even half an hour. Half an hour a night to be with her, even if she was asleep. I wouldn't have minded. It would have been easy. When I think about her and when I speak her name, I think of these things: the good times and wishing I hadn't slept so much. If I were to hear you speak her name, if you could ever manage to, I would probably think of the same things. You are a coward. But worse than a coward, you do not understand anything. You are a coward and you understand nothing. I'm ashamed to know you. Next time, if there is a next time, and in this moment I don't care if there isn't, say her name—say "Sarah", and practise it at home in front of a mirror if you really need to—or say nothing at all and never speak to me again.*'

J said, 'Okay, but . . .'

Simon laughed, and said, 'But I didn't say it. She'd gone. I couldn't believe her lack of understanding. Really, I couldn't, and I still can't. I forgot what it was I was doing, where I was going. Then I remembered the items I had left the house for. I got the items and walked home. I love hearing Sarah's name. It reminds me I'm not crazy. In an internal way, I'm repeating her name constantly, so hearing someone else say *Sarah* makes me feel less alone. I wondered if I should call Nicole and apologise, but then I remembered that there was nothing to apologise for. She hadn't heard my rant. I sat on the settee, where you're sitting now, and I slept.'

'Sarah wasn't murdered, Simon.'

Simon acted as though he hadn't heard.

J said, 'Sarah's birthday must be a strange day for you.'

'You don't understand.'

'And I won't try to. I'm leaving now.'

Simon said, 'Listen, really, what do you know exactly? What was at the root of all that about the lawnmower and the CD? I gave them back, intact.'

'I should've stopped Laura coming here. I could have, but you needed her.'

'So you think you lent her to me? Is that what you're saying?'

'I know about your evenings together. I know she cooked for you. She told me how close you were. There are no secrets.'

'Who said we had a secret?'

'Don't pretend you didn't enjoy it.'

'The evenings or the secret? You're not lucid.'

'The secret. You enjoyed keeping it from me.'

'You really think I was in a position to enjoy anything back then. I didn't. Aren't you leaving now?'

'Yes, I am,' J said.

'Leave then. Go home. I presume you're okay to drive yourself home.'

'I haven't been drinking.'

'That's something then.'

J was back at his not more than half an hour from leaving. He thought Laura might still ask where he went, but she would only ask once if she did. When he opened the front door, he thought again of their old front door coming off in her hands. If it came off again they would at least have something to do. The last time, after she had finished apologising, he left and bought a new door. She wanted to come, but, he reminded her, someone had to wait at the open house. She wasn't thinking properly. He bought a new door, with some money they hadn't even dreamt of saving yet, and it was fitted that evening. She apologised again that night, and he almost lost his temper telling her to stop. But they had something to talk about.

Laura was sitting at the kitchen table.

'Where have you been?'

'Nowhere, walking,' he said.

The following morning, J went upstairs and woke Laura. 'The sun's out. Come on,' he said.

'Come on?'

'Sit outside with me, out the back. I've made coffee.'

'I've just woken.'

'Look, I didn't tell you about the first meal because I preferred your version. I preferred it and I forgot about the truth. It became real because you said it, and because I liked it that way. When we were sitting with Simon yesterday, I felt it was time to tell the truth, the real truth. I didn't think about it. I didn't mean anything by it. I said it, okay, but it doesn't mean I meant it. I heard myself saying it as you heard me. I was as surprised as you. Now come and have some coffee with me. It's getting cold.'

'Okay.' She followed him downstairs. 'You need a haircut,' she said.

'I know.'

He carried the pot of coffee outside and she took two cups and the sugar pot.

'You've cut the grass. How long have you been awake?'

'Not long.'

She said, 'I love the smell. But the morning has to be right, doesn't it? Too hot and it smells dry. Too damp and you feel you're breathing the damp into your lungs. But this is right, isn't it?'

He poured the coffee. 'This is nice.'

'It's not that sunny though. Look at the clouds.'

He looked up and squinted.

'Hope it won't rain,' she said.

'That one looks like . . .' he said, before stopping himself.

'Looks like what? Which one looks like what?'

He pointed out another cloud and told her it looked like a slide. He laughed inwardly at how easily any image could relate to what he had on his mind. The way he was thinking, nothing could shake it from his thoughts, and she had no idea.

'It doesn't look that much like a slide. It looks more like a rattle.'

He laughed aloud. She laughed too, but hers was nothing more than an echo of his.

'Hungry?' she said.

'No,' he said, before he considered the question.

She tucked her hair behind her ears as if to encourage the sun to come out a little more. 'You know, sometimes I have no idea what I want to do and it's almost painful. But now, I have no idea and it's wonderful.'

'Good, but I'm not sure what you mean exactly.'

'I'm not sure either,' she said, and after finishing her cup of coffee, she tried to explain herself. 'This is one of those times that I don't feel as though I need anything.'

'Good.'

'Do you ever feel like you could say something, I don't know, something profound?'

'Go on then,' he said. 'I'd like to hear something.'

'No, I'm not going to say anything, but I feel as though I could, if I were someone else. This would be the right time. My mind is clear. I don't need or want anything.'

'I bet you wouldn't say no to a croissant though,' he said.

'You bought some?'

'No, but I'll go now.'

'No, stay here for some time. When I said I didn't need anything, I meant *anything*,' she said.

They sat there quietly for another fifteen minutes. He went inside to make a pot of tea because she said that's what she wanted. They skipped breakfast and instead went out to the coast for a pub lunch and a walk. On their way home they stopped at a supermarket to fill the car with petrol and buy a few bottles of wine.

'Really wanted a drink in the pub earlier,' he said, catching her looking at the bag.

'I could tell.'

'Do you mind?'

'No, you should drink every now and then,' she said.

The late afternoon sun made the living room come alive. All of the small speckles of dust, agitated under the spotlight that shot from the window right across to the other side of the room, captured their attention while they shared one bottle. He opened another bottle, and she wished, but only lightly, that she knew how much of the first bottle she had drank. He topped up both their glasses before the drinks were finished. She was sure it was an old trick of his. But it hardly mattered anymore, she reminded herself.

'There's a man outside the window,' she said.

'What,' J said, turning to the window.

The man waved as though he'd known them for years. J walked to the door, saying, as he walked, 'Who is he?'

Laura was beside J when he opened the door, and she greeted the man.

'Hello,' the man said. 'Had it that no one was in. It looks dark.'

'We're in,' J said.

'This your place then?' the man said.

'It is,' J said.

'Used to live here.'

'Here?' Laura said. 'You lived here?'

The man nodded. 'Mind if I come in?' he said.

Laura said, 'No, come in,' before J could say anything. Despite the day's sun, it was cold outside.

J and Laura watched the man enter the house. Everything about him was slow. The man's hesitancy started to impress on J and Laura too, and for a minute or so they walked through a few rooms, watching everything, as if a movement of a head threatened to put a crack in the wall.

'Mind leaving me for a tad?' the man said.

'Leaving?' J said.

'It's a lot to see at once, all the people,' the man said.

Laura took J's arm and said, 'Come on.'

They stepped out the front and looked at each other. J went to the man's car. It looked like it had been cleaned that morning. J checked the man had locked it. After some time, the man met them out front.

'Did you find it?' Laura said, smiling.

'What?'

'What you were looking for?'

'I'm not looking for anything. You're both young, you'll find out one day.'

J said, 'What do you mean? And anyway, we're not so young.'

Laura pinched J's elbow, and he moved it away to show she had hurt him. The man smiled.

'You're young, and trust me, you won't be looking for

anything when you're as old as me. Finding requires searching, and searching requires energy. The truth is, you just don't bother.'

The light changed and it was almost too dark to see outside.

'Let's go in,' Laura said, and the men followed.

The man said, 'Okay to smoke?'

'Normally I'd say no, but have one if you want,' Laura said.

The man lit his cigarette, the lighter's flame showing the wrinkles on his face, but that was nothing compared to his hands. J looked at his own hands. The man offered them a cigarette and they both took one. They offered the man a glass of wine, but he refused. The man had the single chair, and J and Laura the double. They could have managed with the single though, sitting as close as they were.

'Let me tell you a story,' the man said. He told them about a friend he'd had, the first girl he ever really knew. 'We were sixteen,' he said. 'She called for me on Saturday mornings with her Labrador. The most beautiful dog I'd ever seen, and still. I liked him from the get-go.' The old man looked up and smiled. 'We used to walk around Highlands Park. Is it still there?'

J and Laura both said they didn't know.

'Maybe they've renamed it; maybe it's gone. Anyway, we'd walk for a couple of hours. Just that. This went on for a few months until she moved away. Let me tell you, I hate that I was too scared. But even the mental picture of her makes me nervous. What am I saying? You get older and you learn to talk, and talk for longer if you forget your point. I'm telling you, or I'm trying to tell you, that regret is unavoidable. I'm trying to tell myself too. Have you ever stuck to anything you've told yourself? Doesn't work, does it? So I'm telling you. You seem like a nice couple. Do you have children? Don't be shy.'

Laura looked up at J.

Her moist eyes worked as a spotlight, so he read his line. 'It never happened,' he said.

'I'm sorry.'

'Don't be. Do you drink tea?' Laura said.

'I got out of the habit after . . . I got out of the habit recently,' the man said.

J made a pot as the man and Laura talked in the living room. When he brought in the tea, Laura was crying.

'All right?' J said.

'Yes,' Laura said.

The man said, 'The colour in the kitchen was cream. I liked it then, but I like it now too, what you've done. The things in there—the cooker, fridge, the work surfaces—they've changed, but they're still in the same places. It's funny, but standing in there didn't make me think of any dishes my mum made us, not to begin with. It took some time. Eventually, I thought of her mashed potato and how I'd practically kill to eat it today. I thought of a few dishes eventually. The thing I thought of first though was having my hair cut, my brother too. She used to sit us beside each other and cut our hair in the kitchen. I'd forgotten, entirely. She once threatened to cut his ear off. He was crying, wiggling around. She didn't warn him she might cut it if he moved. She *told* him she *would* cut it. Soon stopped him.'

'Have the other rooms changed then?' J said.

'All of them,' the man said. He scratched his forehead and said, 'I should go.'

'Stay,' Laura said, but he walked towards the front door.

Laura said, 'Wait. How was your life?'

The man laughed.

'No, really,' she said.

The house turned into a smaller space when the man answered. 'Before today I hardly remembered my childhood. Now I can remember pennies and peanuts, but what for? I don't feel any better. Let me tell you something. No, forget it.'

'Tell us,' Laura said.

'I won't.'

'What about today though, coming here? Was it what you expected? Did you find what you were looking for?' she said.

'Expected? I never expected or wanted a thing. Didn't I tell you that already? Didn't you already ask me that?'

'You were looking for something,' J said.

The man breathed aloud and left them.

After closing the front door, Laura said, 'Poor man.'

'Poor?'

'His wife, recently.'

'That's a shame,' J said.

'It is.'

'He remind you of anyone though?'

'Who? What?' she said.

J smiled.

Laura hit him on the chest and said, 'Don't be nasty.'

J took the cups to the kitchen. He walked back into the living room with a fresh bottle of wine and said, 'If we added up all we've been through and what the people we know have been through, all the significant things, what we know about, what I know about that you don't know I know about, it would seem almost dramatic, wouldn't it? But don't you feel too calm sometimes, almost like we're too still for our own good?'

'I don't know,' she said, trying to ignore a part of his speech that stuck out like hearing a friend's name on the news. *What is it he thinks he knows about me?*

J filled their glasses. He said, 'I'm not saying it's a big thing or anything. Don't think that I'm saying that. I'm saying that that's how it is, how it feels. We're supposed to feel still, I think. Despite everything, we're calm and still a lot of the time, and I mean still in a good way, like a solid chair or table.'

'You're a funny one,' she said, trying to keep things light.

'And so are you,' he said, and she worried he might change and wondered how many glasses he had drank.

'How is that then?' she said in a soft voice.

'You'd have to be funny, wouldn't you, to be with me. We're like two still solid armchairs sat next to each other, being sat on, being moved around, knocked over, pushed from one side of the room to the other, used as goalposts, whatever, but we're still doing all right . . . I think I've had enough. Take it away.'

'Do you feel okay?'

'I'm okay. You don't need to ask every time,' he said.

The way her worry doubled after he stopped drinking always surprised her. She took the bottle through to the kitchen.

'Too tired to cook,' she said.

'Too tired to eat,' he said.

After fifteen minutes, he said he might drink another glass. She poured one for him, one for herself.

'If you wanted one you could've had one,' he said.

'What do you mean?'

'You don't have to wait for me. You didn't have to.'

'I wasn't,' she said.

'You never drink in front of me, but you can, you know.'

'I had a beer in the pub earlier.'

'One beer.'

'I was hardly going to have three, was I?' she said.

He laughed. 'I'm sorry, I'm sorry,' he said.

'No need to say sorry,' she said, not wanting him to go too far that way.

'Let's put an end to this tonight,' he said.

'An end to what?'

'All this recent business. Spending time with Simon and seeing that lonely man makes me want to put an end to it even more than I already did.'

'Go on then,' she said.

'I wasn't thinking us through, and never was. Didn't I say that?' he said.

'Yes.'

'Didn't I tell you that several times?'

'You did, I know.'

'Sure, you've done some things I wish you hadn't, but so have I. They were upsetting, I'm not saying they weren't, but they were inevitable and I always knew they were. This is how I look at it. If I had the choice to be Simon and have the image of a perfect wife and the missed opportunity of a perfect life, or to be me and have an imperfect relationship with someone real, someone I love, then I'd choose this every time.'

She decided he must be more sober than she thought. 'What's this been about then? I could've sworn you said you were leaving me. What's this about?'

‘I said I was thinking things through, and this has been about thinking things through. Just things,’ he said.

‘What things?’ she said.

‘It sounds silly now. I don’t think it now.’

‘Tell me anyway,’ she said, standing.

‘I told you it sounds silly, and I don’t think it anymore. Sit down.’

She remained standing. ‘You need to tell me.’

‘Okay. I became frightened.’

‘Of?’ she said.

He controlled the silence to slow the conversation, as confidently as a conductor of an orchestra. ‘The thought of not leaving anything behind,’ he said.

‘But you’re not frightened anymore? Or are you still? You’re not too old, J, that’s the thing, that’s the truth, but I am. It’s too late for me, but not you. That’s right, isn’t it? Are you still frightened? Because, and look, if you’re still frightened then there’s a chance you’ll go, isn’t there? Are you?’

He stood, and was surprised to find himself so much taller than her. It was a strange thing to be surprised about after all this time.

‘Fear doesn’t leave like that,’ he said.

Her hand gripped his forearm, close to his elbow, as though using him to stand.

‘Are you okay?’ he said.

If the television was on, they didn’t hear it.

ABOUT THE AUTHOR

Samuel Burrows studied Creative Writing at the University of Derby. He now lives in Bulgaria. *The Little Movements* is his debut novel.